Miss Read, or in real life Dora Saint, was a school teacher by profession who started writing after the Second World War, beginning with light essays written for *Punch* and other journals. She then wrote on educational and country matters and worked as a scriptwriter for the BBC. Miss Read was married to a schoolmaster for sixty-four years until his death in 2004, and they have one daughter.

In the 1998 New Year Honours list Miss Read was awarded an MBE for her services to literature. She is the author of many immensely popular books, including two autobiographical works, but it is her novels of English rural life for which she is best known. The first of these, *Village School*, was published in 1955, and Miss Read continued to write about the fictitious villages of Fairacre and Thrush Green until her retirement in 1996. She lives in Berkshire.

Village Affairs

* * *

Miss Read

Illustrated by J. S. Goodall

An Orion paperback

First published in Great Britain in 1977
by Michael Joseph Ltd
This paperback edition published in 2008
by Orion Books Ltd
Orion House, 5 Upper St Martin's Lane,
London WC2H 9EA

An Hachette Livre UK company

A CIP catalogue record for this book is
available from the British Library.

Typeset at the Spartan Press Ltd,
Lymington, Hants

Printed and bound in Great Britain by
Clays Ltd, St Ives plc

The Orion Publishing Group's policy is to use papers
that are natural, renewable and recyclable products and
made from wood grown in sustainable forests. The logging
and manufacturing processes are expected to conform to the
environmental regulations of the country of origin.

www.orionbooks.co.uk

To
Anthea and Mac
With love

CONTENTS

* * *

PART ONE

The Rumours Fly

PART TWO

Fairacre Hears the News

PART THREE

Fate Lends a Hand

PART ONE

The Rumours Fly

* * *

1. FOREBODINGS

It is an undisputed fact that people who choose to live in the country must expect to be caught up, willy-nilly, in the cycle of the seasons.

Spring-cleaning is done to the accompaniment of the rattle of tractors as they drill up and down the bare fields outside. Lambs bleat, cuckoos cry, blackbirds scold inquisitive cats, while upstairs the sufferers from spring influenza call hoarsely for cold drinks.

Summer brings its own background of sights and sounds and the pace of village life quickens as fêtes follow cricket matches, and outings, tennis parties and picnics crowd the calendar.

There is not quite so much junketing in the autumn, for harvest takes pride of place, and both men and women are busy storing and preserving, filling the barns and the pantry shelves.

It is almost a relief to get to winter, to put away the lawn mower, to burn the garden rubbish, and to watch the ploughs at work turning the bright corn stubble into dark chocolate ribs ready for winter planting, while the rooks and peewits flutter behind, sometimes joined by seagulls when the weather is cruel elsewhere.

For each of us in the country, our own particular pattern of life forms but a small part against the general background of the seasons. If you are a schoolmistress, as I am, then the three terms echo in miniature the rural world outside. The Christmas term brings the arrival of new children to the school, harvest festival and, of course, the excitement of Christmas itself.

The Spring term is usually the coldest and the most germ-ridden, but catkins and primroses bring hope of better times, and summer itself is the crown of the year.

It is good to have this recurring rhythm, this familiar shape of the year. We know – to some extent – what to expect, what to welcome, what to avoid.

But there is another aspect of country life which is not so steady. There are certain topics which crop up again and again. Not, to be sure, as rhythmically as primroses and harvest, but often enough over the years to give us a little jolt of recognition. There is the matter of the village hall, for instance. Is it needed or not needed? And then there is the parlous state of the church organ and its eternal fund. And Mrs So-and-so is expecting again for the twelfth – or is it the thirteenth? – time, and something must be done about her house, or her husband, or both.

It is rather like watching a roundabout at a fair. The galloping horses whirl by, nostrils flaring, tails streaming, and then suddenly there is an ostrich, strange and exotic in its plumage among the everyday beasts. The merry-go-round twirls onward and we begin to sink back again into our pleasant lethargy when, yet again, the ostrich appears and our interest is quickened once more. So it is with these topics which disappear for a time whilst we are engrossed with everyday living, and then reappear to become the chief matters of importance, our talking points, things which have startled us from our normal apathy and quickened our senses.

Just such a recurring topic is the possible closure of Fairacre School. I have been headmistress here for a number of years, and talk of closing it has cropped up time and time again, diverting attention from the Church Organ Fund and the village hall as surely as the ostrich does from the horses. Naturally, after a week or two, the excitement dies down, and we continue as before with feelings of relief, until the next crisis arrives.

The cause varies. The true difficulty is that our numbers at the school scarcely warrant two teachers. One-teacher schools are considered undesirable, rightly, I think, and have been closing steadily in this area. Every now and again, the word goes round that Fairacre School really only needs one and a half teachers, and this half-teacher problem cannot be overcome, although one has the pleasing fancy that a great deal of ruler-gnawing in county offices goes on while the matter is being given consideration.

Usually, Providence steps in. A new family of six children appears, and is joyously added to the register. Cross parents refuse to send their young children by bus to the next village, or some other benign agency gets to work, and the matter of Fairacre School's closure is shelved once more.

I had become so used to the ostrich appearing, that I confess I could scarcely distinguish him from the galloping horses.

Until one evening, when Mr Annett, the headmaster of neighbouring Beech Green School, startled me with his disclosures.

As well as being a headmaster, George Annett is choirmaster of St Patrick's, Fairacre. On Friday evenings he drives over from Beech Green, a distance of some three miles, to officiate at choir practice.

For a small village we have quite a flourishing choir. Two of the stalwarts are Mr Willet, part-time caretaker of the school, sexton, grave-digger and general handyman to the whole village, and Mrs Pringle, our lugubrious school cleaner, whose booming contralto has been heard for long – far too long, according to the ribald young choristers – resounding among the rafters of St Patrick's roof.

On this particular Friday, George Annett called at the school house where I was busy putting away the week's groceries and trying to recover from the stunning amount I appeared to owe for about ten everyday items.

'Have a drink,' I said. 'I reckon I need a brandy when I see the price of butter this week.'

'A spot of sherry would be fine,' said George. 'Not too much. Can't arrive at church smelling of alcohol, or Mrs P. will have something to say.'

'Mrs Pringle,' I told him, with feeling, 'always has something to say. And usually something unpleasant. That woman positively invites assault and battery.'

'Heard the latest? Rumour has it that my school is being enlarged.'

'I've heard that before. And Fairacre's closing, I suppose?'

George studied his sherry, ignoring my flippancy. His grave face sobered me.

'It rather looks like it. The chap from the office is coming out next week to see me. Don't know why yet, but this rumour has reached me from several sources, and I believe something's in the wind. How many children do you have at the moment?'

'We're down to twenty-eight. Miss Edwards has fifteen infants. I have the rest. Incidentally, she's going at the end of term, so we're in the throes of getting a new appointment.'

'No easy task.'

'No. I expect we'll have to make do with a number of supply teachers until next term when the girls are appointed from college.'

George Annett put down his glass and rose to his feet. 'Well, I'll let you know more when I've seen Davis next week. I can't say I want a bigger school. We'll have the upheaval of new building going on, and a lot of disgruntled parents who don't want their children moved away.'

'Not to mention disgruntled out-of-work teachers.'

'You won't be out of work for long,' he smiled. 'Perhaps you'll be drafted to Beech Green?'

'And where should I live? No doubt the school and the school house would be sold together pretty quickly, and I certainly can't afford to buy either. I'm going to need a sub from the needlework tin, as it is, to pay for this week's groceries!'

George laughed, and departed.

I might have ignored this rumour, as I had so many others, if it had not been for Mrs Pringle.

She arrived at the school house on Saturday morning with a

nice plump chicken, of her own rearing, in the black oilcloth bag which accompanies her everywhere.

'Have a cup of coffee with me,' I invited.

'I don't mind if I do,' replied Mrs Pringle graciously.

I recalled a forthright friend who used to reply to this lacklustre acceptance by saying: 'And I don't mind if you don't!' But, naturally, I was too cowardly to copy her.

I took the tray into the garden, Mrs Pringle followed with the biscuit tin. Spring at Fairacre is pure bliss and I gazed fondly at the almond blossom, the daffodils and the faintest pink haze of a copper beech in tiny leaf.

'I see you've got plenty of bindweed in your border,' said Mrs Pringle, bringing me back to earth with a jolt. 'And twitch. No need to have twitch if you weeds regular.'

It sounded like some nervous complaint brought on by self-indulgence – a by-product of alcoholism, perhaps, or drug addiction. However, the sun was warm, the coffee fragrant, and I did not intend to let Mrs Pringle deflect me from their enjoyment.

'Have a biscuit,' I suggested, pushing the tin towards her. She selected a chocolate bourbon and surveyed it with disapproval.

'I used to be very partial to these until they doubled in price pretty nearly. Now I buy Osborne. Just as nourishing, and don't fatten you so much. At least, so Dr Martin said when he gave me my diet sheet.'

'A diet sheet?'

'Yes. I'm to lose three stone. No starch, no sugar, no fat, and no alcohol – though the last's no hardship, considering I signed the pledge as a child.'

'Then should you be eating that biscuit, and drinking coffee with cream in it?'

'I'm starting tomorrow,' said Mrs Pringle, taking a swift bite at the biscuit.

'I see.'

'You've heard about our school shutting, I suppose?' said the lady, her diction somewhat blurred with biscuit crumbs.

'Frequently.'

'No, the latest. My cousin at Beech Green says they're going to build on to Mr Annett's school, and send our lot over there in a bus. Won't suit some of 'em.'

A vague feeling of disquiet ran through me. Mrs Pringle was so often right. I remembered other dark warnings, airily dismissed by me, which had been proved correct as time went by.

Mrs Pringle dusted some crumbs from her massive chest.

'Some seems to think the infants will stay here,' she went on, 'but I said to Florrie – that's my cousin at Beech Green, and a flighty one she used to be as a girl, but has steadied down wonderful now she's got eight children – I said to her, as straight as I'm saying to you now, Miss Read, what call would the Office have to keep open all that great school for a handful of fives to sevens? "Don't make sense," I said, and I repeat it now: "It just don't make sense."'

'No indeed,' I agreed weakly.

'Take the heating,' continued Mrs Pringle, now in full spate. She held out a large hand, as though offering me the two tortoise stoves in the palm. 'Sacks of good coke them stoves need during the winter, not to mention blacklead and brushes and a cinder pail. They all takes us taxpayers' money. Then there's brooms and dusters, and bar soap and floor cloths, which costs a small fortune—'

'And all the books, of course,' I broke in.

'Well, yes,' said Mrs Pringle doubtfully, 'I suppose they needs *books*.' She spoke as though such aids to learning were wholly irrelevant in a school – very small beer compared with such things as scrubbing brushes and the other tools of her trade.

'But stands to reason,' she continued, 'that it's cheaper for all the whole boiling lot to go on the bus to Beech Green, though what the petrol costs these days to trundle them back and forth, I shudders to think.'

'Well, it may not happen yet,' I said, as lightly as I could. 'We've had these scaremongering tales before.'

'Maybe,' said Mrs Pringle, rising majestically, and adjusting the black oilcloth bag over her arm. 'But this time I've heard it from a good many folk, and when have our numbers at Fairacre School ever been so low? I don't like it, Miss Read. I feels in my bones a preposition. My mother, God rest her, had second sight, and I sometimes thinks I take after her.'

I devoutly hoped that Mrs Pringle's premonition meant nothing, but could not help feeling uneasy as I accompanied her to the gate.

'You wants to get rid of that bindweed,' was her parting shot, 'before it Takes Over.'

That woman, I thought savagely as I collected our cups, always has the last word!

By Monday morning my qualms had receded into the background, as they had so often before. In any case, everyday problems of the classroom successfully ousted any future threats.

Patrick had been entrusted with a pound note for his dinner money and had lost it on the way. He was tearful, fearing awful retribution from his mother.

'It was in my pocket,' he sniffed, mopping his tears with the back of his hand. 'All scrunched up, it was, with these 'ere.'

He produced four marbles, a stub of pencil, a grey lump of bubble gum and a jagged piece of red glass.

'You'll cut yourself on that,' I said. 'Put it in the wastepaper basket.'

He looked at me in alarm. A fat tear coursed unnoticed down his cheek.

'But it's off my brother's rear lamp,' he protested.

'Well, put it in this piece of paper to take home,' I said, giving in. 'And put all that rubbish on the side table. Now *think*, Patrick. Did you take the pound note out of your pocket on the way?'

'Yes, he did, miss,' chorused the class.

'He showed it to me,' said Linda Moffat. 'He said he betted I didn't have as much money.'

'That's right,' agreed Ernest. 'And it was windy. Blowing about like a flag it was. I bet it's blown over the hedge.'

'And some old cow's eaten it.'

'Or some old tramp's picked it up.'

'Or some old bird's got it in its nest.'

At these helpful surmises, Patrick's tears flowed afresh.

'You must go back over your tracks, Patrick, and search,' I told him. 'And someone had better go with him. Two pairs of eyes are better than one.'

Silence descended upon the class. Arms were folded, chests stuck out, and expressions of intense capability transformed the countenance of all present. What could be better than escaping from the classroom into the windy lane outside?

'Ernest,' I said, at last.

There was a gust of expelled air from those waiting lungs, and a general slumping of disappointed forms.

Ernest and Patrick hastened from the room joyfully, almost knocking over Joseph Coggs who was entering with a bunch of bedraggled narcissi. He looked bemused.

'I bin and brought you some flowers,' he said, holding them up.

'My auntie brought them on Saturday, but my mum says they'll only get knocked over, so you can have them.'

'Well, thank you. Fetch a vase.'

When he returned, I added: 'You're late, you know, Joseph.'

His lower lip began to droop and I feared that we should have yet another pupil in tears.

'A policeman come,' he said.

Everyone looked up. Here was real drama!

'From Caxley,' faltered Joseph. Bright glances were exchanged. This was better still!

'He wanted to see my dad, but he was in bed. My mum give me these flowers and said to clear off while she got Dad up. The policeman's waiting in our kitchen.'

'Well, there's no point in worrying about that,' I said reassuringly. 'Your mother and father will see to it.'

The class looked disappointed at the dismissal of such an enthralling subject. What spoilsports teachers are, to be sure!

By the time prayers had been said, a hymn sung and the rest of the pupils' dinner money safely gathered into my Oxo tin, the hands of the great wall clock stood at a quarter to ten. Patrick and Ernest were still at large in the village, and no doubt enjoying every minute of it.

'We're having a mental arithmetic test this morning,' I announced, amidst a few stifled groans, 'and I shall want someone to give out the paper.'

At that moment, there was a cry from the back of the room, and Eileen Burton stumbled down the aisle with a bloodied handkerchief clapped to her streaming nose.

This is a frequent occurrence and we all know what to do.

'Lay down, girl!' shouted one. I should like to have given – not for the first time – a short lecture on the use of verbs 'to lie' and 'to lay', but circumstances were against me. As it was, I fetched the box of paper handkerchiefs and assisted the child to a prone position by the stove.

'Shall I get the cold water?'

'Do she need a cushion, miss?'

'She wants a bit of metal down her neck, miss.'

I fetched the cutting-out scissors, a hefty chunk of cold steel, and put them at the back of her neck, substituting, at the same time, a wad of paper tissues for the deplorable handkerchief. Eileen remained calm throughout, accustomed to the routine.

We left her there, and set about the test.

'Number down to twenty,' I told them. Would we never get started?

There was a clanging noise as feet trampled over the iron scraper in the lobby. Ernest and Patrick entered, wind-blown and triumphant, Patrick holding aloft a very dirty pound note.

'We found it, miss!' they cried. 'Guess where?'

'In the hedge?'

'No.'

'In the duck pond?' shouted someone, putting down his pen.

'No.'

'In your pocket after all?'

'No.'

By now, pens were abandoned, and it was plain that the mental arithmetic test would be indefinitely postponed unless I took a firm hand.

'That's enough. Tell us where.'

'In a cow pat. So stuck up it was, it couldn't blow away. Weren't it *lucky*?'

They thrust the noisome object under my nose.

'Wipe it,' I said faintly, 'with a damp cloth in the lobby, then *bring it back*. Don't let go of it for one second. Understand?'

By now it was a quarter past ten and no work done.

'First question,' I said briskly. Pens were picked up, amidst sighing.

'If a man has twelve chickens,' I began, just as the door opened.

'And about time too,' I said wrathfully, expecting Ernest and Patrick to appear. 'Get into your desks, and let's get some work done!'

The mild face of the vicar appeared, and we all rose in some confusion.

2. NEWS OF MINNIE PRINGLE

The Reverend Gerald Partridge has been vicar of this parish for many years. I have yet to hear anyone, even the most censorious chapel-goer, speak ill of him. He goes about his parish duties conscientiously, vague in his manner, but wonderfully alert to those who have need of his sympathy and wisdom.

In winter, he is a striking figure, tramping the lanes in an ancient cape of dramatic cut, and sporting a pair of leopard skin gloves, so old that he is accompanied by little clouds of moulting fur whenever he uses his hands. It is commonly believed that they must have been a gift from some loving, and possibly beloved churchgoer, in the living before he came to Fairacre. Why otherwise would he cling to such dilapidated articles?

Fairacre School is a Church of England School, standing close to St Patrick's and the vicarage. The vicar is a frequent visitor, and although I have heard the ruder boys mimicking him behind his back, the children are extremely fond of him, and I have witnessed them attacking a stranger who once dared to criticize him.

'I'm sorry to interrupt,' he said, 'but I was just passing and thought I would have a word with you.'

'Of course.'

I turned to the class. 'Turn over your test papers and write out the twelve times table,' I directed. Long-suffering glances were exchanged. Trust her to want the twelve times! One of the nastiest that was! Their looks spoke volumes.

'What on earth is the matter with that child?' asked the vicar,

13

in a shocked tone, his horrified gaze upon the prone and blood-ied figure of Eileen Burton.

'Just a nose-bleed,' I said soothingly. 'She often has them.'

'But you should have a key,' cried Mr Partridge, much agit-ated, 'a *large* key, to put at the nape of the neck—'

'She's got the cutting-out scissors—' I began, but he was now too worried to heed such interruptions.

'My mother always kept a large key hanging in the kitchen for this sort of thing. We had a parlour maid once, just so afflicted. What about the key of the school door? Or shall I run back to the vicarage for the vestry key? It must weigh quite two pounds, and would be ideal for the purpose.'

His face was puckered with concern, his voice sharp with anxiety.

At that moment, Eileen stood up, dropped the paper hand-kerchief in the wastepaper basket, and smiled broadly.

'Over,' she announced, and put the scissors on my desk.

'Take care, dear child, take care!' cried the vicar, but he sounded greatly relieved at this recovery. He picked up the cutting-out scissors. 'A worthy substitute,' he conceded, 'but it would be as well to get Willet to screw a hook into the side of one of the cupboards for a key. I can provide you with one quite as massive as this, I can assure you, and I really should feel happier if you had one on the premises.'

I thanked him, and asked what it was he wanted to tell me.

'Simply a rumour about the school closing. I wanted you to know that I have had no official message about such a possibil-ity. I pray that I may *never* have one, but should it be so, please rest assured that I should let you know at once.'

'Thank you. I know you would.'

'You have heard nothing?'

'Only rumours. They fly around so often, I don't let them bother me unduly.'

'Quite, quite. Well, I must be off. Mrs Partridge asked me to pick up something at the Post Office, but for the life of me I can't remember what it is. I wonder if I should go back and ask?'

'No doubt Mr Lamb will know and have it waiting for you,' I suggested.

Mr Partridge smiled with relief. 'I'm sure you're right. I will call there first. No point in worrying my wife unnecessarily.'

He waved to the children, and made for the door.

'I won't forget to look out a suitable key,' he promised. 'My mother would have approved of having one handy at all times. First aid, you know.'

The door closed behind him.

'First question,' I said. 'If a man had twelve chickens—'

Although I had told the vicar that I was not unduly bothered by the rumours, it was not strictly true. Somehow, this time, as the merry-go-round twirled, the ostrich had a menacing expression as it appeared among the galloping horses. Perhaps, I told myself, everything seemed worse because I had heard the news from several sources in a very short space of time.

After school, I pottered about in the kitchen preparing a salad, which Amy, my old college friend, was going to share that evening. She had promised to deliver a pile of garments for a future jumble sale, and as James, her husband, was away from home, we were free to enjoy each other's company.

Apart from a deplorable desire to reform my slack ways, Amy is the perfect friend. True, she also attempts to marry me off, now and again, to some poor unsuspecting male, but this uphill job has proved in vain, so far, and I think she knows, in her heart, that she will never be successful.

It was while I was washing lettuce that Mr Willet arrived with some broad bean plants.

'I saw you'd got some terrible gaps in your row, miss. Bit late perhaps to put 'em in, but we'll risk it, shall us?'

I agreed wholeheartedly.

He departed along the garden path, and I returned to the sink.

'*No rose in all the world*' warbled Mr Willet, '*until you came.*'

Mr Willet has a large repertoire of songs which were popular at the beginning of the century. They take me back, in a flash, to the musical evenings beloved of my parents. Mercifully, I can only remember snippets of these sentimental ballads, most of which had a lot of 'ah-ah-ah'-ing between verses, although a line or two, here and there, still stick in my memory.

'*Dearest, the night is over*' (or was it 'lonely'?)

'*Waneth the trembling moon*' and another about living in a land of roses but dreaming of a land of snow. Or maybe the other way round? It was the sort of question to put to Mr Willet, I decided, when Amy arrived, and Mr Willet and the ballads were temporarily forgotten.

'Lovely to be here,' sighed Amy, after we had eaten our meal. She leant back in the armchair and sipped her coffee. 'You really do make excellent coffee,' she said approvingly. 'Despite the haphazard way you measure the beans.'

'Thank you,' I said humbly. I rarely get praise from Amy, so that it is all the more flattering when I do.

She surveyed one elegant hand with a frown.

'My nails grow at such a rate. I always remember a horrifying tale I read when I was about ten. A body was exhumed, and the poor woman's coffin was full of her own hair and immensely long finger nails.'

'Horrible! But it's common knowledge that they go on growing after death.'

'A solemn thought, to imagine all those dark partings on Judgement Day,' commented Amy, patting her own neat waves. 'Well, what's the Fairacre news?'

I told her about the school, and its possible closure.

'That's old hat. I shouldn't worry unduly about that, though I did hear someone saying they'd heard that Beech Green was to be enlarged.'

'The grape vine spreads far and wide,' I agreed.

'But what about Mrs Fowler?'

'Mrs Fowler?' I repeated with bewilderment. 'You mean that wicked old harridan who used to live in Tyler's Row? Why, she left for Caxley years ago!'

'I know she did. That's why I hear about her from my window cleaner who lives next door to her, poor fellow. Well, she's being courted.'

'Never! I don't believe it!'

Amy looked pleasantly gratified at my reactions.

'And what's more, the man is the one that Minnie Pringle married.'

This was staggering news, and I was suitably impressed. Minnie Pringle is the niece of my redoubtable Mrs Pringle. We Fairacre folk have lost count of the children she has had out of wedlock, and were all dumb-founded when we heard that she was marrying a middle-aged man with children of his own. As far as I knew, they had settled down fairly well together at Springbourne. But if Amy's tale were to be believed, then the marriage must be decidedly shaky.

'Mrs Pringle hasn't said anything,' I said.

'She may not know anything about it.'

'Besides,' I went on, 'can you imagine anyone falling for Mrs Fowler? She's absolutely without charms of any sort.'

'That's nothing to do with it,' replied Amy. 'There's such a thing as incomprehensible attraction. Look at some of the truly dreadful girls at Cambridge who managed to snaffle some of the most attractive men!'

'But Mrs Fowler—' I protested.

Amy swept on. 'One of the nastiest men I ever met,' she told me, 'had four wives.'

'What? All at once? A Moslem or something?'

'No, no,' said Amy testily. 'Don't be so headlong!'

'You mean headstrong.'

'I know what I mean, thank you. You rush *headlong* to conclusions, is what I mean.'

'I'm sorry. Well, what was wrong with this nasty man you knew?'

'For one thing, he cleaned out his ears with a match stick.'

'Not the striking end, I hope. It's terribly poisonous.'

'*Whichever* end he used, the operation was revolting.'

'Oh, I agree. Absolutely. What else?'

'Several things. He was mean with money. Kicked the cat. Had Wagner – of all people – too loud on the gramophone. And yet, you see, he had this charm, this charisma—'

'Now there's a word I never say! Like "Charivari". "Punch or the London" one, you know.'

Amy tut-tutted with exasperation. 'The point I have been trying to make for the last ten minutes,' shouted Amy rudely, '*against fearful odds*, is that Minnie Pringle's husband must see something attractive in Mrs Fowler.'

'I thought we'd agreed on that,' I said. 'More coffee?'

'Thank you,' said Amy faintly. 'I feel I need it.'

The fascinating subject of Mrs Fowler and her admirer did not crop up again until the last day of the spring term.

Excitement, as always, was at fever-pitch among the children. One would think that they were endlessly beaten and bullied at school when one sees the joy with which they welcome the holidays.

Miss Edwards, who had been my infants' teacher for the past two years, was leaving to get married at Easter, and we presented her with a tray, and a large greetings card signed by all the children.

The vicar called to wish her well, and to exhort the children to help their mothers during the holidays, and to enjoy themselves.

When he had gone, I contented myself with impressing upon them the date of their return, and let them loose. Within minutes, the stampede had vanished round the bend of the lane, and I was alone in the schoolroom.

I always love that first moment of solitude, when the sound

of the birds is suddenly noticed, and the scent of the flowers reminds one of the quiet country pleasures ahead. Now, freed from the bondage of the clock and the school timetable, there would be time 'to stand and stare', to listen to the twittering of nestlings, the hum of the early foraging bees, and the first sound of the cuckoo from the coppice across the fields.

Spring is the loveliest time of the year at Fairacre, when everything is young, and green, and alive with hope. Soon the house martins would be back, and the swifts, screaming round and round the village as they selected nesting places. Then the swallows would arrive, seeking out their old familiar haunts – Mr Roberts' barn rafters, the Post Office porch, the loft above the vicar's stables – in which to build their nests.

Someone had brought me a bunch of primroses as an end of term present. Holding the fragrant nosegay carefully, I made my way through the school lobby towards my home across the playground, full of anticipation at the happiness ahead.

The door scraper clanged. The door opened, and Mrs Pringle, her mouth set grimly, confronted me.

'Sorry I'm a few minutes late,' she began, 'but I'm In Trouble.'

'In Fairacre, this expression is commonly used to describe pregnancy, but in view of Mrs Pringle's age, I rightly assumed that she used the term more generally.

'What's wrong?'

'It's our Minnie,' said Mrs Pringle. 'Up my place. In a fair taking, she is. Can't do nothing with her. I've left her crying her eyes out.'

'Oh, dear,' I said weakly, my heart sinking. Could Amy have heard aright?

I smelt my sweet primroses to give me comfort.

'Come to the house and sit down,' I said.

Mrs Pringle raised a hand, and shook her head.

'No. I've come to work, and work I will!'

'Well, at least sit on the bench while you tell me.'

A rough plank bench in the playground, made by Mr Willet, acts as seat, vaulting horse, balancing frame and various other things, and on this we now rested, Mrs Pringle with her black oilcloth bag on her lap, and the primroses on mine, in the hedge dividing the playground from the lane, a blackbird scolded as Tibby, my cat, emerged from the school house to see why I was taking so long to get into the kitchen to provide her meal.

'That man,' said Mrs Pringle, 'has up and left our Minnie. What's more, he's left his kids, and hers, and that one of theirs, to look after, while he gallivants with that woman who's no better than she should be.'

'Perhaps he'll come back,' I suggested.

'Not him! He's gone for good. And d'you know who he's with?'

'No,' I said, expecting to be struck by lightning for downright lying.

'You'll never guess. That Mrs Fowler from Tyler's Row.'

I gave a creditable gasp of surprise.

'The scheming hussy,' said Mrs Pringle wrathfully. A wave of

20

scarlet colour swept up her neck and into her cheeks, which were awobble with indignation.

'It's my belief she knew he had an insurance policy coming out this month. After his money, you see. Well, it wouldn't have been his looks, would it?'

I was obliged to agree, but remembered Amy's remark about the plain girls and the young Adonises at Cambridge. Who could tell?

'But, top and bottom of it all is – how's Minnie to live? Oh, I expect she'll get the Social Security and Family Allowance, and all that, but she'll need a bit of work as well, I reckons, if she's to keep that house on at Springbourne.'

'Won't he provide some money?'

'That'll be the day,' said Mrs Pringle sardonically. 'Unless Min takes him to court, and who's got the time and money to bother with all that?'

Mrs Pringle's view of British justice was much the same as her views of my housekeeping, it seemed, leaving much to be desired.

'If she really needs work,' I said reluctantly, 'I could give her half a day here cleaning silver, and windows, and things.'

Mrs Pringle's countenance betrayed many conflicting emotions. Weren't her own ministrations on my behalf enough then? And what sort of a hash would Minnie make of any job offered her? And finally, it was a noble gesture to offer her work anyway.

Luckily, the last emotion held sway.

'That's a very kind thought, Miss Read. Very kind indeed.'

She struggled to her feet, and we stood facing each other. Tibby began to weave between our legs, reminding us of her hunger.

'But let's hope it won't come to that,' she said. I hoped so too, already regretting my offer.

Mrs Pringle turned towards the lobby door. 'I'll let you know what happens,' she said, 'but I'll get on with a bit of scrubbing now. Takes your mind off things, a bit of scrubbing does.'

She stumped off, black bag swinging, whilst Tibby and I made our way home.

3. COULD IT BE ARTHUR COGGS?

The policeman from Caxley, who had called upon the Coggs household, was making inquiries, we learnt, about the theft of lead in the neighbourhood.

Scarcely a week went by but the *Caxley Chronicle* reported the stripping of lead from local roofs around the Caxley area. Many a beautiful lead figure too, which had graced a Caxley garden for generations, was spirited away under cover of darkness, lead water tanks and cisterns, lead guttering, lead piping, all fell victim to a cunning band of thieves who knew just where to collect this valuable metal.

It so happened that the Mawnes had an ancient summer house, with a lead roof, in their garden.

Their house had been built in the reign of Queen Anne, and the octagonal summer house, according to Mr Willet, who considered it unsafe and unnecessarily ornate, was erected not long afterwards, although it was, more likely, the conceit of some Victorian architect. It was hidden from the house by a shrubbery, and nothing could have been easier for thieves than to slip through the hedge from the fields adjoining the garden to do their work in privacy.

The lead was not missed until a thundery shower sent cascades of water through the now unprotected roof into the little room below. A wicker chair and its cushion were drenched, a water colour scene, executed by Mrs Mawne in her youth, became more water than colour overnight, and a rug, which Mr Mawne had brought back from Egypt on one of his bird-watching trips, and which he much prized, was ruined. Added to all this was the truly dreadful smell composed of wet timber and the decaying bodies of innumerable insects, mice, shrews and so on, washed from their resting places by the onrush of rain.

Fairacre was shocked at the news. It was one thing to read in the pages of the respected *Caxley Chronicle* about lead being stolen from villages a comfortable distance from their own. It was quite another to find that someone had actually been at work in Fairacre itself. What would happen next?

Mr Willet voiced the fears of his neighbours as he returned from choir practice one Friday night.

'What's to stop them blighters pinching the new lead off the church roof? Cost a mint of money to put on. It'd make a fine haul for some of these robbers.'

A violent storm, some years earlier, had damaged St Patrick's sorely. Only by dint of outstanding efforts on the part of the villagers, and never-to-be-forgotten generosity from American friends of Fairacre, had the necessary repairs been made possible. The sheets of lead, then fixed upon much of the roof, had formed one of the costliest items in the bill. No wonder Fairacre folk feared for its safety, now that marauders had visited their village.

'They wouldn't dare to take the Lord's property,' announced Mrs Pringle.

'I don't think they care much whose property it is,' observed Mr Lamb from the Post Office. 'It's just how easy they can turn it into hard cash.'

'My sister in Caxley,' replied Mrs Pringle, still seeking the limelight, 'told me the most shocking thing happened all up the road next to hers.'

'What?' asked Mr Willet. The party had reached the Post Office by now and stopped to continue the conversation before Mr Lamb left them.

Twilight was beginning to fall. The air was still and scented with the flowers in cottage gardens.

Mrs Pringle looked up and down the road before replying.

Her voice was low and conspiratorial. Mr Willet and Mr Lamb bent their heads to hear the disclosure.

'Well, these lead thieves came one night and went along all the outside lavatories, and cut out every bit of piping from the cistern to the pan.'

'No!'

'They did. As true as I'm standing here!'

'What! Every house?'

Mrs Pringle shifted her chins uncomfortably upon the neck of her cardigan.

'Not quite all. Mr Jarvis, him what was once usher at the Court, happened to be in his when they reached it, so they cleared off pretty smartly.'

'Did they catch 'em?'

'Not one of 'em!' pronounced Mrs Pringle. 'Still at large, they are. Quite likely the very same as took Mr Mawne's lead off the summer house.'

'Could be,' agreed Mr Lamb, making towards his house now that the story was done. 'Thought I heard as Arthur Coggs might be mixed up with this little lot.'

'Now, now!' said Mr Willet, holding up a hand in a magisterial gesture. 'No hearsay! It's not right to go accusing people. Us doesn't know nothing about Arthur being connected with lead stealing.'

'He's connected with plenty that's downright dishonest,' rejoined Mr Lamb, with spirit. 'Dammit all, man, he's done time, he's a poacher, he's been had up, time and time again, for stealing. And he ought to be had up for a lot of other things, to my mind. Wife-beating for one. And dodging the column for another. Why, that chap hasn't done a day's work for weeks, and all us old fools keeps him by giving him the dole and the family allowances. Makes my blood boil!'

'We knows all that,' agreed Mr Willet, taking a swipe at a passing bat with a rolled-up copy of Handel's *Messiah*. 'But you just can't pin everything that's crooked on Arthur Coggs.'

'Why not?' asked Mrs Pringle belligerently. 'More times than not you'd be right!'

And on this note the friends parted.

Human nature being what it is, there were far more people in Fairacre who shared Mrs Pringle's view than Mr Willet's.

Arthur Coggs was the black sheep of the village, and his wife greatly pitied. He was supposed to be a labourer, although his neighbours stated roundly that labour was the last thing Arthur looked for. He occasionally found a job on a building site, carrying a hod, or wheeling a barrow slowly from one place to the next. But he rarely stayed long. Either he became tired of the work, or more often, his employer grew tired of paying him to do nothing.

The greater part of his money went on beer, and he was a regular customer at the Beetle and Wedge in Fairacre. He and his family had once occupied a tumbledown cottage, one of four in Tyler's Row, now made into one long attractive house occupied by a retired schoolmaster from Caxley and his wife.

The Coggs family had been rehoused in a council house which was fast becoming as dilapidated as their last abode. Mrs Coggs, with a large family to cope with, and very little money with which to do it, struggled to tidy the house and garden, but never succeeded. Over the years she had grown thinner and greyer. Her highest hopes were that Arthur would stay sober, and that he would provide more housekeeping money. So far, her hopes had not been realized.

Now and again, Arthur would appear to have money in his pocket and this she felt certain was the result of some dishonest dealings. Arthur had appeared in the Court at Caxley on many occasions, and his list of previous convictions, handed up for the Bench to study, included such offences as theft, receiving goods knowing them to have been stolen, shoplifting, burglary and house-breaking.

Mrs Coggs knew better than to question Arthur about any unusual affluence. A black eye, or painful bruises elsewhere would have been the outcome. But experience had given her some cunning and she had sometimes been able to abstract a pound note or some change from his pocket, when he was fuddled with drink.

Pity for Arthur's wife had prompted several people in Fairacre to employ her dissolute husband over the years. Mr Roberts, the local farmer, had taken him on as a farm hand, only to find that eggs vanished, one or two hens disappeared, as well as sacks of potatoes and corn. The other men complained that they were doing Arthur's work as well as their own and they were right. Mr Roberts dispensed with Arthur's services.

Mr Lamb had tried to employ him as a jobbing gardener, but again found that vegetables were being taken and the jobs set him were sketchily done, and the local builder's patience snapped when he caught Arthur red-handed, walking home with a pocketful of his tools.

The plumber at Springbourne, whose soft heart had been touched by the sight of Mrs Coggs and her four children all in tears one morning as he passed through Fairacre, was moved to take on Arthur for a week's trial. By Wednesday he discovered that a considerable amount of copper piping had vanished, and Arthur was sacked once again.

Virtually, he was unemployable, and soon realized that he was far better off collecting his social security allowance and other moneys disbursed by a benevolent government, and indulging his chronic laziness at the same time.

He was known to be in tow with some equally feckless and dishonest men in Caxley and, in fact, Arthur frequently acted as look-out man when the more daring of the gang were breaking-in. His wages for this kind of work were in proportion to the loot obtained, but always far less than the share each burglar received.

'You didn't take much risk, chum,' they told him. 'Piece of cake being look-out. You can reckon yourself lucky to get this bit.'

And Arthur agreed. As long as it helped to keep him in beer, there was no point in arguing.

For a while, immediately after the discovery of the loss of Mr Mawne's roofing lead, Fairacre folk were extra careful about making their homes secure. People actually shut their front doors on sunny days, instead of leaving them hospitably open for neighbours to enter. They began to hunt for door keys, long disused, and some very funny places they were found in after the passage of time. Mr Willet, after exhaustive searching, admitted that he found his front door key at the bottom of a biscuit tin full of nuts, bolts, screws, hinges, padlocks, latches, tacks, brass rings, and other useful impedimenta vital to a handyman.

His neighbour found his on top of the cistern in the outside lavatory. The two Misses Waters, Margaret and Mary, who had a horror of burglars but so far relied on a stout bolt on both back and front doors, now scoured their small cottage in vain for the keys they had once owned. It was Margaret who remembered eventually, at three o'clock one morning, that they had hidden them under the fourth stone which bordered their brick path, when they were going away for a brief holiday some years earlier. At first light, she crept out, and unearthed them, red with rust. She remained in a heady state of triumph all day.

Mr Lamb, it seemed, was the only householder in Fairacre who locked up and bolted and barred his premises methodically every night. But then, as people pointed out, as custodian of the Queen's mail he'd have to see things were done properly or he'd soon get the boot. No one gave him credit for his pains, and to be honest, Mr Lamb was sensible enough not to expect any. But at least he was spared the searching for keys, for his own hung, each on its hook and carefully labelled, ready for its nightly work.

For a time, even the children caught the fever and became aware that it was necessary to be alert to dishonesty. One Caxley market day, Linda Moffat and Eileen Burton arrived each with a door key on a string round their necks.

'My mum's gone on the bus to buy some material for summer frocks,' said Linda, 'and she may not be back when I get home.'

'And mine's gone to buy some plants,' announced Eileen. 'Ours never come to nothing.'

'If they never come to nothing,' I said severely, 'then they must have come to something. Say what you mean.'

The child looked bewildered. 'I did, miss. Our seeds never come—'

'*Your seeds did not come up*,' I said, with emphasis.

'That's what I said.'

'You did not say that,' I began, and was about to embark, for the thousandth time, on an elementary grammar lesson, when Mr Willet intervened. He had been listening to the exchange.

'Your mum's seeds never come up,' he said forcefully, 'because she used that plaguey compost muck out of a bag. She wants to mix her own, tell her, with a nice bit of soft earth and dung and a sprinkle of sharp sand. Tell her they'll never come to nothing in that boughten stuff.'

I gave up, and turned to the marking of the register.

It came as no surprise to the good people of Fairacre when they heard that a week or two after the visit of the police to the Coggs' house Arthur Coggs was to appear in Court charged, together with others, with stealing a quantity of lead roofing, the property of H.A. Mawne Esq.

At the time of the theft, the *Caxley Chronicle* had given some prominence to the affair, enlarging upon Mr Mawne's distinction as an ornithologist, and reminding its readers that the gentleman had frequently contributed nature notes to the paper's columns. News must have been thin that week for not only was Mr Mawne given an excessive amount of type, but a photograph was also included, taken by one of the younger staff against the background of the depleted summer house.

Even the kindest readers were at a loss to find something nice to say about the likeness, and the subject himself said it looked to him like an explosion in a pickle factory, adding tolerantly that maybe he really looked like that and had never realized.

'There's three other chaps,' Mr Willet told me. 'Two of 'em is Bryants – that gipsy lot – and the third's a real bad 'un from Bent. I bet he was the ringleader, and that poor fool of an Arthur Coggs told him about the roof here. I still reckons we ought to keep watch on the church, but the vicar says we must trust our brothers.'

'He's a good man,' I commented.

'A sight too good, if you ask me. "There's brothers and brothers," I told him. I wouldn't want any of them four for brothers, and I wouldn't trust them no further than that coke pile, idle thieving lot.'

'We don't know that they're guilty yet,' I pointed out.

'I do,' said Mr Willet, picking up his screwdriver.

Later, I overheard a conversation in the playground as I strolled round holding my mug of tea. It was a glorious May morning. The rooks cawed from the elm trees as they went back and forth feeding their hungry nestlings, and the children were sitting on the playground bench, or had propped themselves against the school wall, legs outstretched, as they enjoyed the sunshine.

Joseph Coggs sat between Ernest and Patrick, all three oblivious of the condition of their trouser seats in the dust.

'Saw your dad in the paper,' said Ernest.

'Ah,' grunted Joseph.

'Bin pinchin', ain't he?' said Patrick.

'Dunno.'

'That's what the paper said.'

Joseph scratched a bite on his leg and said nothing.

'That's what the copper come about,' said Ernest to Patrick.

'Is he in prison?' asked Patrick conversationally of Joseph.

'No,' shouted Joseph, scrambling to his feet. His face was red, and he looked tearful. He rushed away towards the boys' lavatories, obviously craving privacy, and I approached his questioners.

They gazed up at me innocently.

'You should stand up when ladies speak to you,' I told them, not for the first time. They rose languidly.

'And don't let me hear you upsetting Joseph with questions about his father. It's none of your business and it's unkind anyway.'

'Yes, miss,' they replied, trying to look suitably chastened.

One or two of the other children hovered nearby, listening to my brief homily, and I was conscious of meaningful glances being exchanged. It was difficult to be critical. After all, the Arthur Coggs affair was the main subject of spicy conjecture in their homes at the moment, and it was hardly surprising that they shared their parents' interest.

That afternoon when the sun was high in the heaven, and the downs were veiled in a blue haze of heat, I decided that a nature walk was far more beneficial to my pupils than a handiwork lesson.

As the sun was so hot, we kept to the lanes, in and around the village, which are shaded by fine old trees. The hawthorn hedges were sprouting young scarlet shoots, and in the cottage gardens the columbines were out. The children call them 'granny's bonnets', and they are exactly like the beautifully goffered and crimped sun bonnets that one sees in old photographs.

Some of the lilac flowers were beginning to turn rusty, and the old-fashioned crimson peonies were beginning to droop their petals in the heat, but the scent was heavy, redolent of summer and a whiff of the long days ahead.

The children straggled along in a happy and untidy crocodile, chattering like starlings and waving greetings to friends and relations as they passed.

Fairacre, I told myself, was the perfect place to live and work, and early summer found it at its most beautiful. I stopped to smell a rose nodding over a cottage gate, and became conscious of voices in the garden. Two neighbours were chatting over their boundary hedge.

'And if it isn't Arthur Coggs, then who is it?' asked one.

I sighed, and let the rose free from my restraining hand.

Every Eden seemed to have its serpent, Fairacre included.

4. MRS PRINGLE HAS PROBLEMS

With the departure of the infants' teacher, Miss Edwards, we were back in the familiar circumstances of looking for a second member of staff.

As it happened, only two new children arrived for the summer term, both five-year-olds, making the infants' class seventeen in all. Altogether we had now thirty children on roll, and although this might sound a laughably small number to teach compared with some of the gigantic classes in overcrowded urban primary schools, yet there were considerable difficulties.

I struggled alone for two weeks before a supply teacher could be found.

It meant a proliferation of groups working in the one classroom, and an impossible situation when one tried to play games, or choose a story or a song, which could be enjoyed by five-year-olds and eleven-year-olds at the same time. I always feared that some accident might happen, when the sole responsibility rested on me to get help and to look after the rest of the school at the same time. It was a worrying time and I was mightily relieved when Mrs Ansell arrived to share the burden.

She was a cheerful young woman in her thirties whom I had met once or twice at teachers' meetings in Caxley. She had a young son of two, and had not taught since his birth, but her mother lived nearby in Caxley, and was willing to mind the child if Mrs Ansell wanted to do occasional supply teaching.

All went well for a fortnight, and the children were settling down nicely under their new regime, when the blow fell. She rang me one evening to say that her mother had fallen down in the garden and damaged her hip. She was in Caxley hospital, and of course quite unable to look after Richard.

I expressed my sympathy, told her we could manage, and hung up.

Now what, I wondered? Supply teachers are as rare and as precious as rubies. Most of those local few who were in existence lived in Caxley and preferred to attend the town schools. I had been lucky enough to get Mrs Ansell because she paricularly wanted to teach infants, liked country schools, and had her own car.

'I shall have to ring the Office again in the morning,' I told Tibby gloomily. 'And what hope there?'

Tibby mewed loudly, but not with sympathy. Plain hunger was the cause, and I obediently dug out some Pussi-luv and put it on the kitchen floor. I then supplied my own supper plate with bread and cheese.

It was while I was eating this spare repast that I thought of Amy. She has helped us out on occasions, and there is no one I would sooner have as my companion at Fairacre School.

'Are you in the middle of your dinner?' was Amy's first remark.

'It's only the last crumb of bread and cheese,' I assured her.

'Is that all you have had?'

'Yes. Why?'

'I really do think you should be a little less slapdash with your meals,' said Amy severely. 'And on your lap, I suppose. It's ruination to the digestion, you know, these scrambled snacks.'

'Well, never mind that,' I said impatiently, and went on to tell her our troubles.

'Could you?' I finished.

'I could come on Monday,' said Amy, 'not before, I'm afraid, as I'm helping Lady Williams with the bazaar for the Save The Children Fund on Friday.'

'Come and save my children instead.'

'And it can't be for long,' went on Amy, 'as I have Vanessa coming some time next month.'

'But you could come for a week or two?'

'Probably three weeks. James is off to Persia on some trade mission or other, and then to Australia, I believe, unless it was New Zealand. They're so close, one gets confused.'

'I believe they are thousands of miles apart, and they get pretty stroppy about being muddled up. It's like the Scandinavian countries, isn't it? Do you know which is top and bottom of that craggy looking piece of coastline?'

'No, I don't. But I remember it was always a great help to trace the outline on the way home in the train. The movement was invaluable round the fiords.'

'You are a darling to come,' I said, reverting to the main topic. 'I'll ring the Office in the morning and get things straight, and let you know the result. It really is murder trying to cope alone. One grazed knee or a pair of wet knickers is enough to stop us all in our tracks.'

'Never fear,' cried Amy, 'help is on its way!'

'The relief of Mafeking,' I told her, 'will be nothing to it.'

Jubilantly, I hung up.

The Office gave its blessing to my arrangements, and we all awaited Amy's coming with varying degrees of pleasure.

My own feeling was of unadulterated relief. The vicar, who has a soft spot for Amy, said it would be delightful to see her again, and how very generous she was with her time when one considered that she had a husband and a house to look after.

Mr Willet was equally enthusiastic. 'I can ask her about those pinks cuttings I give her,' he said. 'Always a bit tricky pinks are, if the soil's not to their liking. I'd dearly love to go over to Bent to keep an eye on 'em, but I don't want to push meself forward.'

I said I felt sure that Amy would welcome his advice, and he retired to the playground humming cheerfully.

Mrs Pringle greeted the news with modified rapture. Amy is too well-dressed, drives too large a car, and altogether has an aura of elegant affluence which Mrs Pringle disapproves of in a teacher. I think she feels that anyone as comfortably placed as Amy should do a little voluntary work for some deserving charity, but to take on a teaching job smacks too much of depriving some poor wretch of her rightful dues.

Since taking to her slimming diet, Mrs Pringle seemed to be even more martyr-like than usual. She received the news of Amy's arrival on Monday with a resigned sigh.

'Best get both gates wide open,' she said, 'for that great car of hers. I take it you'll tell the children to keep off of it? It's a big responsibility havin' an expensive motor like that on the premises, and I haven't got eyes in the back of my head.'

I reassured her on that point.

'And last time she come, she didn't eat no potatoes I noticed. Now that's a bad example to the children. We tells 'em to eat up all they've got, and then they sees their teachers pickin' and choosin'. Just drop a word, Miss Read. She's your friend after all.'

'How's the dieting?' I asked, hoping to change the subject.

Mrs Pringle's gloom deepened. 'That Dr Martin's getting past it. Fairly snapped my head off when I went to get weighed, just because I've only lost two pounds in a month! I told him straight: "Well, at least I've *lost* it. There's no call to get so white and spiteful. Anyone'd think I'd *put on* two pounds"! He calmed down a bit then, and made me write down all I'd eaten since Sunday.'

'Could you remember?'

'Most of it. And when I give him the list, he shouted out so loud that Mrs Pratt's baby started hollering in the waiting room.'

'Why, what was wrong?'

'You may well ask. He shouted: "I said no cakes, no bread, no potatoes, and no sugar"! And I said to him: "How's a body to drink tea without sugar? And what's tea time without a slice of cake? And what's a dinner plate look like without a nice little pile of potatoes?" He never answered. Just went a bit pink, and hustled me out, telling me to do what he'd said. No sense to him these days. Too old for the job, if you ask me.'

'But he's right, you know. You won't lose weight unless you cut out all those lovely fattening things.'

'I don't call them *fattening*,' said Mrs Pringle, with immense dignity. 'They're *sustaining*! A woman what works as hard as I do needs nourishment. The days I've given up me bread and that, I've felt proper leer. Me knees have been all of a tremble. With this job to do, let alone my own home, I needs the food.'

There seemed little to add. Mrs Pringle shuffled off, limping slightly, a sure sign that her bad leg was giving trouble, as it always does in times of stress.

As she went, I noticed she did up a button on her cardigan which had burst from its buttonhole under excessive strain. The two pounds had not been lost from that portion of her anatomy obviously.

Come to think of it, I pondered, watching her massive rear vanish into the lobby, it would be difficult to say just where she had lost those pounds.

The hot weather continued, showing May in all her glory. In my garden the pinks began to break, shaking their shaggy locks from the tight grey cap which held them.

On the front of the school house, the ancient Gloire de Dijon rose, planted by one of my predecessors, turned its fragrant flat-faced flowers to the sunshine in all its cream and pink splendour.

The hay crop looked as though it would be heavy this year, and the bees were working hard. A field of yellow rape made a blaze of colour across one of Mr Roberts' stretches of land, and it was this, I suspect, that attracted so many bees to the area.

The copper beech was now in full leaf, and the box edging to the garden beds gave off its peculiar aromatic smell as the noonday sun drew out all the delicious scents of summer.

The school room door was propped open with a large knobbly flint, turned up by the plough in the neighbouring field. The sounds and scents wafted in, distracting the children from their work, so that I often took them all into the grass under the trees, and let them listen – or not – to a story. The daddy-long-legs floated round us in the warm air, small birds chattered and squeaked in the branches above, and only the sound of Mr Roberts' tractor in the distance gave any hint of the village life which was going on around us. They were lovely sessions, refreshing to body and mind, and we always returned to the classroom in a tranquil state of mind.

Amy arrived on Monday morning, wearing a beautiful pale pink linen suit, but with her usual foresight had brought with her a deep rose-pink overall to ward off such infant room hazards as sticky fingers, spilt milk, and chalk dust.

Some of the children knew her already, and it was not long before her calm efficiency had made friends of them all. I closed the infants' room door with a sigh of relief, and set out to catch up with many neglected lessons with my older children.

Things went swimmingly all week until Friday morning.

'Guess who I saw at the bus stop in Caxley,' said Amy, trying to adjust her hair by the reflection from 'The Light of the World' behind my chair.

'Haven't a clue,' I replied.

'Why don't you have a mirror somewhere? I see there isn't one in the lobby either. Where do you do your hair?'

'At home.'

'But surely, when you've been in the playground on a windy day, you – and the children, for that matter – need to tidy up.'

'We manage.'

'By just leaving things, I suppose,' said Amy. 'It's too bad of you, you know. The children should be set an example of neatness. And did you know that the hem is coming down on that frock?'

'I had a suspicion. There was an ominous tearing sound when I caught my heel in it this morning, but no time to investigate.'

'Dreadful!' murmured Amy, more in sorrow than anger. She does try so hard to improve me, with practically no success.

'You were telling me,' I said, 'about someone at the bus stop. Miss Clare?'

'At eight-thirty in the morning? Don't be silly.'

'Who then?'

'Mrs Fowler and Minnie Pringle's husband, whatever he's called.'

'What? Waiting for the bus to Springbourne?'

'It looked remarkably like it.'

I pondered upon this snippet of news. 'Do you think they might be going to collect his children from Minnie's?'

'It would be a jolly good thing if they did,' said Amy forthrightly, 'but I doubt it. They've managed quite happily without them, as far as one can see, so why suddenly want a family reunion now?'

'It certainly seems odd,' I agreed. 'Perhaps Mrs Pringle will be able to throw light on the matter.'

Sure enough, when Mrs Pringle arrived for her after school duties, it was quite apparent, from the important wobbling of her chins, that she had great news to impart.

'Well, I've got that Minnie of mine back again. I've left her grizzling in the kitchen and the children are in the garden. I've dared them to put a foot on the flower beds, unless they want to be skinned alive. I can't say fairer than that to them.'

'What's the matter this time?' I asked. Amy who had picked up her handbag ready to depart, put it down again and perched on the front desk to observe the scene.

Mrs Pringle looked at her with some dislike, but aquiver as she was with her momentous news, she decided to ignore her presence and tell all.

'That man had the cheek to come out to Minnie's this morning, with that woman who's no better than she should be, and I'll not soil my lips by repeating her name, and ask for his furniture back.'

'But can he? Isn't it the marital home, or whatever they call it in Court?'

'Whether he can or he can't,' boomed Mrs Pringle, 'he's done it. And that Mrs Fowler—'

'With whose name you wouldn't soil your lips,' I remembered silently.

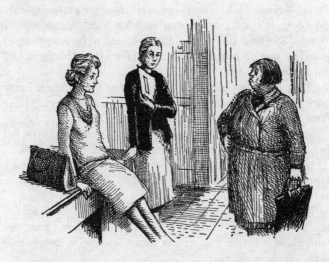

'Well, she was at the bottom of it. It was that cat as put him up to it. And her nephew had his van waiting by Minnie's gate to put the stuff in. All planned and plotted you see. And off they drove, leaving our Minnie without a frying pan in the house.'

'Nothing at all?' I said horrified.

Mrs Pringle tutted with impatience.

'No, no, they never took *the lot*, I'll give 'em that, but they took two armchairs, and the kitchen table, and no end of china, and the upstairs curtains, and some cooking pots and the frying pan, so of course Minnie and the kids have had no dinner.'

I could not quite see why the frying pan was the only utensil needed to cook the family's food, but this was no time to go into all that, and I was beginning to feel very sorry for poor luckless Minnie, and for Mrs Pringle too, when her next remark cooled my sympathy.

'So it looks to me, Miss Read, as Minnie will be very glad to take up your offer of some work. She's got all that stuff to buy anew, and money's very tight anyway. I told her to come up and see you to arrange things some time.'

'Thank you,' I said faintly. It was an appalling prospect, and I cursed myself for ever making such an idiotic suggestion. I avoided meeting Amy's gaze. She appeared to be struggling to hide her very ill-timed amusement. Like Queen Victoria, my amusement was nil.

'Well, I'd better get on with my tidying up and then hurry back to see what damage them little varmints of Minnie's have done. When shall I tell her to come?'

'She'd better come one evening,' I said. 'There's no hurry, tell her, and if she gets a post elsewhere I shall quite understand.'

Amy suffered a sudden fit of coughing which necessitated a great deal of play with her handkerchief. At times, she can be very tiresome.

'Right!' said Mrs Pringle, shaking out a clean duster from her black oilcloth bag. 'I'll let her know. But I wouldn't trust her with glass, if I were you, or any china. She's a bit clumsy that way.'

She went into the infants' room and vanished from our sight.

'Come and have tea with me,' I said to Amy.

'No, I really must get back, but I couldn't possibly leave before knowing the outcome of this morning's activities.'

We walked out into the sunlit playground. Overhead the swifts screamed and whirled, and the air was deliciously fresh after the classroom.

'Looks as though I'm saddled with that ghastly Minnie,' I remarked.

'You should have been firm from the outset,' replied Amy.

'I didn't get much chance,' I protested. 'She practically told me she was coming. What on earth could I do?'

'You could have said that you had offered the job to someone else, and it had been accepted.'

'What? In Fairacre? Be your age, Amy! Everyone knows I

haven't a job to offer! It's as much as I can cope with having Ma Pringle bullying me about the house. I don't want more.'

'You should have thought about that earlier,' said Amy primly. 'I'm always telling you how you rush headlong into things.'

'Well, don't keep rubbing it in,' I retorted crossly. 'It's quite bad enough having to face the possibility of Minnie wrecking my home weekly, without enduring your moralizing.'

Amy laughed, and patted my shoulder.

'What you need is a nice husband to protect you from yourself.'

She slid into the driving seat.

'That I don't,' I told her, through the car window. 'I've quite enough troubles already, without a husband to add to them.'

Amy shot off with an impressive turn of speed, and I waved until my maddening old friend had disappeared round the bend in the lane.

5. Hazards Ahead

One Friday evening, George Annett called in on his way to St Patrick's. I could see at once that he was the bearer of bad tidings.

'There's definitely something in the wind,' he said, in answer to my queries. 'I've had several chaps from the Office measuring the school and offering me a temporary classroom to be erected across the playground, complete with wash-basins and lavatories.'

'When?'

'No one can say definitely. Obviously, they're just making sure I can cope with the extra numbers. It may never happen. You know how these things hang on.'

'I remember Dolly Clare telling me that poor Emily Davis, who was head at Springbourne, had this closure business hanging over her for nearly ten years.'

'There you are then! Don't get steamed up yet. But I thought I'd let you know the latest. Had any luck with applicants for the teaching post?'

'Not yet. Amy is coping for a little longer, then it will be another supply until the end of term, if I'm lucky.'

George laughed, and rose to go across to his duties. 'You will be.' He patted my shoulder encouragingly. 'Cheer up! I'd take a bet on Fairacre School remaining as it is for another thirty years.'

'I wonder. Anyway, there's a managers' meeting soon, and perhaps we'll learn something then.'

'Ask Mrs Pringle what's going on,' shouted George, as he went down the path. 'She'd be able to tell you.'

At that moment the lady was approaching, also on her way to choir practice, and had obviously heard the remark.

I was amused to notice George's discomfiture, as he wished her 'Good evening' in a sheepish fashion.

The night was hot, and I could not sleep – a rare occurrence for me.

There was a full moon, and the room was so light that it was impossible to lie still, and equally impossible to draw the curtains on such a torrid night.

The longer I stayed awake, the more I worried. What would become of me if the school closed? I had no doubt that I should be treated honourably by the education authority. Whatever teaching post I was offered would provide me with my present salary, but that was the least of my worries.

Not for the first time, I blessed my single state. I had only myself to fend for, and I thought of other teachers who were widowed with young children, or those who supported aged parents, or invalid relatives, and whose salary had to be stretched much farther than my own. Amy often told me that I led a very selfish life and perhaps it was true, but when one was faced with a situation such as that which I now contemplated, there were compensations. No one depended on me. No one offered me disturbing advice. No one would blame me for any decision I took, however disastrous it turned out to be.

I left my hot and rumpled bed, and hung out of the window. The shining rose leaves glittered in the bright moonlight. The sky was clear, and the evening star hung low over the village, as brilliant as a jewel.

Here was the heart of my grief. To leave this – my well-loved school house, and its garden, shady with trees planted by other teachers, long dead, but remembered by me daily for their works, which still endured.

I could truthfully say that I relished every day that I spent in

Fairacre. It was not only a beautiful place, backed by the downs, open, airy, and dominated by St Patrick's spire thrusting high above the thatched and tiled roofs around it. It was also a friendly place, as I soon found when I had arrived as a newcomer some years earlier.

The thought of leaving Mr Willet, Mr and Mrs Partridge, the Mawnes – even Mrs Pringle – was unbearable. My life was so closely bound with theirs, in fact, so closely woven with all those living in the village that I should feel as weak and withered as an uprooted plant if circumstances forced me to go.

As for the children, to part with them would be the hardest blow. I loved them all, not in a sentimental fashion but because I admired and respected their sound country qualities. I loved their patience, their docility, their efforts to please. Certainly, at times, these very virtues exasperated me. Then I would find them unduly slow, complacent and acquiescent, but when I took stock I had to admit that it was often impatience on my part which roused my wrath. How could I ever leave them?

I returned to my bed, and now it was practical matters which bedevilled me. Why on earth hadn't I bought a house for myself, instead of living in a fool's paradise in the school one? The times I had thought about it – and the times Amy had admonished me on the same subject – were beyond counting.

But somehow, I had let matters drift. I had never seriously thought of leaving Fairacre, apart from the odd urge to make a change which sometimes hit me in the spring. Even then, just reading the advertisements in the *Times Educational Supplement* had usually been enough to quench my brief ardours. To slide gently from middle age to retirement in Fairacre seemed such a serene and mellow way to face the future. Of course, I realized that one day, when I had left, someone else would live in my dear house and teach in the school, but it all seemed so far away that I was lulled into a dream-like state of bliss.

Now had come the rude awakening. It was E.M. Delafield, I believe, who said that she wanted seven words on her tombstone:

'*I expected this, but not so soon.*'

They echoed my own thought absolutely.

All the cocks in Fairacre were crowing before I fell into an uneasy sleep.

It was the following evening, when I was making plans for an early night, that I saw, with horror, the untidy figure of Minnie Pringle coming up the path.

I think it is uncommonly sensible and prudent of Minnie to buy her clothes at local jumble sales, and I have often recognized old garments of mine among her wardrobe. But what irks me is the way she wears them without the slightest attempt to adapt them to her skinny figure.

She is particularly fond of a dilapidated fur coat which was once Mrs Mawne's. It is a square garment, made from square pieces of moulting fur. A great many squares are parting from their neighbours, and as the whole thing swamps Minnie, it would have seemed reasonable to remove one row of squares to make it fit, or at least to mend the slits and tie a belt round it. As it is, Minnie's hands are hidden about six inches up the sleeves, the hem, which is coming undone, reaches her calves, and the rest of the tent-like object swings about round Minnie's frame like a scarecrow's coat on a broomstick.

On this occasion, as the evening was warm, I was spared Mrs Mawne's ex-coat, for Minnie was wearing a shiny mauve blouse over a wrap-around skirt whose pattern seemed vaguely familiar to me. On her bare feet were black patent evening sandals with high heels ornamented with diamanté studs.

I braced myself for the interview and invited her in.

'Auntie says as you could do with some help,' began Minnie, once settled in an armchair.

'Would two hours a week suit you?'

I had given some thought to this problem of my own making, and had decided that, with some contriving, I could find her work within her limited ability which would not conflict too obviously with Mrs Pringle's duties. It was going to be a delicate matter trying to keep her off her aunt's preserves, such as cleaning my few pieces of silver and washing the kitchen floor with as much care as one would sponge a baby's face, and I guessed that my efforts were probably doomed to failure at the outset. But surely, in two hours even Minnie could not do much harm.

Also, two hours of work were really all I could afford to pay on top of Mrs Pringle's weekly dues. I awaited Minnie's reaction with mixed feelings.

Minnie scratched her tousled red locks with a silver-varnished nail of inordinate length.

'Same pay as auntie?' she inquired at length.

'Yes.'

'OK. What wants doin'?'

'I'll show you in a minute,' I said, feeling that we were going along rather fast. 'When can you come? I gather you have some work already.'

'You can say that again,' said Minnie, lying back and putting her sandals on the coffee table. 'I goes to Mrs Partridge Mondays – the vicar fixed that.'

My heart bled for poor Mrs Partridge, at the mercy of her husband's Christian charity. The havoc Minnie could cause in that fragile collection of old glass, Hepplewhite chairs and china cabinets made one shudder to contemplate.

'Then I goes to Mrs Mawne on Wednesday morning, but that's all scrubbin'. Mr Mawne don't want no one to touch his butterfly drawers and stuffed birds and that, though I offered to give 'em a good dusting. He's a funny chap, ain't he?'

I forbore to comment, but my opinion of both Mr and Mrs Mawne's good sense rose considerably.

'And Thursday evenings I does out the hall, 'cos Auntie says she's getting a bit past it, and the committee gentlemen said it was all right for me to do it, though I don't know as I shall stick it long.'

'Why not?'

'Mucky. Bits of sausage roll and jam tart squashed between the floor boards, and the sink gets stopped up with tea leaves.'

'Don't they use tea bags?'

Minnie's mouth dropped open. She looked as though she had been coshed. I began to feel alarmed, but at last she spoke.

'Cor!' she whispered. 'You're a marvel! I'll tell 'em that! It's the cricket tea ladies as does it, I reckons, though them scouts and cubs isn't above mucking things up in spite of them oaths they take. Tea bags is the answer. Of course it is.'

I said I was glad to have been of help, and wondered how soon I should be ostracized by all those who managed the village hall kitchen.

'Is that all the work you do?'

'I has to keep my own place tidy at Springbourne,' said Minnie, looking suddenly truculent.

I hastened to apologize. 'Of course, of course! I meant any more work in Fairacre.'

Minnie sat up, removed her sandals from the table top, and surveyed her grubby toe nails.

'I likes to keep Saturday free.'

'Naturally. I shouldn't want you to give up your weekends. What about Friday afternoons?'

'I shops on Fridays.'

'Wednesday then?'

'Auntie comes up here Wednesdays.'

'Oh, of course. Tuesday any good?'

'I goes to Springbourne Tuesdays, 'cos it's double Green Shield Stamp day at the shop.'

'What's wrong with Monday?'

'The vicar.'

I was beginning to get desperate. Did Minnie want work or did she not? Heaven alone knew I would be happy to dispense with her services, but having got so far I felt I must soldier on. I changed my tactics.

'Well, Minnie, when *could* you come?'

'Friday afternoon.'

I took a deep breath. 'But I thought you said you went shopping on Friday.'

'Not till six o'clock. It's late night Caxley.'

I controlled a sudden desire to scream the place down.

'Very well then, let's say from two until four on Friday afternoon. Or one-thirty to three-thirty, if that suits you better.'

'Is that harpast one?'

'Yes,' I said weakly. Whoever had had the teaching of Minnie Pringle deserved deep sympathy, but not congratulation.

There was silence as Minnie scratched her head again, and thought it out. 'Well, that's fine and dandy. I'll come up harpast one and do two hours, and go at – what time did you say?'

'Harpast – *half past* three,' I said faintly. 'I shall be back from school soon after that.'

'What about me money then?' She sounded alarmed.

'I shall leave it on the mantelpiece,' I assured her, 'just as I do for Mrs Pringle. Now, come and look at the work.'

I proposed that she took over window-cleaning and the upstairs brasswork, and bath and basins. This meant that she would be out of Mrs Pringle's way, and could not do too much damage.

I showed her where the dusters and cleaning things were kept, and she looked doubtfully at the window-cleaning liquid.

'Ain't you got no meths and newspaper? It does 'em a treat. Keeps the flies off too.'

I said shortly that this was what I used, and that I disliked the smell of methylated spirits.

'My uncle drinks it,' she said cheerfully. 'Gets real high on it. They picks 'im up regular in Caxley, and it's only on meths!' She sounded proud of her uncle's achievements.

We returned downstairs.

'You want the grandfather clock done? I could polish up that brass wigger-wagger a treat. And the glass top.' There was a gleam in her mad blue eyes which chilled me. '*Never* touch that clock!' I rapped out, in my best school-marm voice.

'OK.' said Minnie, opening the door. 'See you Friday then, if not before.'

I watched her totter on the high heels down the path, still trying to remember where I had seen that skirt before.

'Heaven help us all, Tibby,' I said to the cat, who had wisely absented herself during Minnie's visit. 'Talk about sowing the something-or-other and reaping the whirlwind! I've done just that.'

I felt the need for an early bedtime more keenly than ever. Just before I fell asleep, I remembered where I had seen Minnie's skirt before.

It had once been my landing curtain. I must say, it looked better on Minnie than many of her purchases.

Notice of the managers' meeting arrived a few days after Minnie's visit. It was to be held after school as usual, on a Wednesday. There was nothing on the agenda, I observed, about possible closure of the school. Could it be village rumours once again?

The vicar called at the school on the afternoon following the receipt of our notices. He was in a state of some agitation.

'It's about the managers' meeting. I'm in rather a quandary. My dear wife has inadvertently invited all the sewing ladies that afternoon, so the dining-room will be in use. The table, you know, so convenient for cutting out.'

'Don't worry,' I said. 'We could meet here, if it's easier.'

We usually sit in comfort at the vicar's mahogany dining-table, under the baleful eye of an ancestor who glares from a massive gilt frame behind the chairman's seat. Sometimes we have met in the drawing-room among the antique glass and the china cabinets.

'And the drawing-room,' went on Mr Partridge, looking anguished, 'is being decorated, and everything is under shrouds – no, not *shrouds* – furniture covers – no, *loose* covers – no, I don't think that is the correct term either—'

'Dust sheets,' I said.

His face lit up with relief. 'What a *grasp* you have of everything, dear Miss Read; no wonder the children do so well! Yes, well, you see my difficulty. And my study is so small, and very untidy, I fear. I suppose we could manage something in the hall, but it is rather draughty, and the painters are in and out, you know, about their work, and like to have their little radios going with music, so that I really think it would be *better*, if you are sure it isn't inconveniencing—'

'Better still,' I broke in, 'have it in my dining-room. There's room for us all.'

'That would be quite perfect,' cried the vicar, calming down immediately. 'I shall make a note in my diary at once.'

He sighed happily, and made for the door. 'By the way, no more news about the possible closing. Have you heard anything?'

'Not a word.'

'Ah well, no news is good news, they say. We'll hear more

perhaps on Wednesday week. I gather that nice Mr Canterbury, who is in charge of Caxley Office, is coming out himself.'

I thought that sounded ominous but made no comment.

'No,' said the vicar, clapping a hand to his forehead. 'I don't mean *Canterbury*, do I? Now, what is that fellow's name? I know it's a cathedral city. Winchester? Rochester? Dear, oh dear, I shall forget my own soon.'

'Salisbury,' I said.

'Thank you. I shall put it in my diary against Wednesday week. I shouldn't like to upset such an important fellow.'

He vanished into the lobby.

'It's more likely,' I thought, 'that the important fellow will upset us.'

6. THE MANAGERS' MEETING

Amy's last week at Fairacre School arrived all too soon, and I was desolate. She was such good company, as well as being an efficient teacher, that I knew I should miss her horribly.

'Well, I'd stay if I could,' she assured me, 'but Vanessa arrives next week, and I hope she'll stay at least a fortnight. She's rather under the weather. There's a baby on the way. Or *babies*, perhaps!'

'Good heavens! Do they think it will be twins?'

'The foolish girl has been taking some idiotic nonsense called fertility tablets, so it's quite likely she'll give birth to half a dozen.'

'But surely the doctors know what they're doing?'

'Be your age,' said Amy inelegantly. She studied the lipstick with which she had been adorning her mouth. 'I must have had this for years. It's called "Tutankhamen Tint".'

'It can't date from that time.'

Amy sighed. 'The Tutankhamen Exhibition, dear, which dazzled us all some years ago. Everything was Egyptian that year, if you remember. James even bought me a gold necklace shaped like Cleopatra's asp. Devilish cold it is too, coiled on one's nice warm bosom.'

'I'm glad about Vanessa's baby,' I said. 'I'll look forward to knitting a matinée jacket. I've got a pattern for backward beginners that always turns out well. Is she pleased?'

'After eleven in the morning. Before that, poor darling, she is being sick. Tarquin is terribly thrilled, and already planning a mammoth bonfire for the tenants on the local ben, or whatever North British term they use for a mountain in Scotland.'

'He'll have to build six bonfires if your fears prove correct.'

'He'd be delighted to, I have no doubt. He's a great family man, and I must say he's very, very sweet to Vanessa. They seem extremely happy.'

She snapped shut her powder compact, stood back and surveyed her trim figure reflected murkily in 'The Light of the World'.

'I think I might present Fairacre School with a pier-glass,' she said thoughtfully.

'It would never get used,' I told her, 'except when you came.'

We went to let in the noisy crowd from the playground.

Mrs Pringle's slimming efforts seemed to be having little result, except to render her even more morose than usual. I did my best to spare her, exhorting the children to tidy up carefully at the end of afternoon school, and putting away my own things in the cupboards instead of leaving them on window sills and the piano top, as I often do.

Luckily, in the summer term, the stoves do not need attention, but even so, it was obvious that she was finding her work even more martyr-making than before. I was not surprised when she did not appear one morning, soon after Amy's departure, and a note arrived borne by Joseph Coggs. He pulled it from his trouser pocket in a fine state of stickiness.

I accepted it gingerly. 'How did it get like this, Joe?'

'I gotter toffee in me pocket.'

'What else?'

'I gotter gooseberry.'

'Anything else?'

'I gotter bitter lickrish.'

'You'd better turn out that pocket!'

'I ain't gotter—'

'And if you say: "I gotter" once more, Joseph Coggs, you'll lose your play.'

'Yes, miss. I was only going to say: "I ain't gotter thing more."'

He retired to his desk, after putting his belongings on the side table, and I read the missive.

Dear Miss Read,

Have stummuck upset and am obliged to stay home. Have had terrible night, but have taken nutmeg on milk which should do the trick as it has afore.

Clean clorths are in the draw and the head is off of the broom.

Mrs Pringle

I called to see my old sparring partner that evening. She certainly looked unusually pale and listless.

'I'm rough. Very rough,' was her reply to my inquiries. 'And there's no hope of me coming back to that back-breaking job of mine this week.'

'Of course not. We'll manage.'

Mrs Pringle snorted. 'But what I mind more is not doing out that dining-room of yours for the managers tomorrow.'

'I'll do it. It's not too bad.'

She gave me a dark look. 'I've seen your sort of housework. Dust left on the skirting boards and the top of the doors.'

'I don't suppose any of the managers will be running their fingers along them,' I said mildly. 'Has the doctor been?'

'I'm not calling him in. It's him as started this business.'

'How do you mean?'

'This 'ere diet. Drinking lemon juice first thing in the morning. That's what made my stummuck flare up.'

'Then leave it off!' I cried. 'Dr Martin wouldn't expect you to drink it if it upset you!'

'Oh, wouldn't he? And the price of lemons what it is too! I bought a bottle of lemon juice instead. And that's just as bad.'

She waved a hand towards a half-empty bottle on the sideboard, and I went to inspect it. It certainly smelled odd.

'Is it fresh?'

Mrs Pringle looked uneasy. 'I bought it half-price in Caxley. The man said they'd had it in some time.'

'Chuck it away,' I said. 'It's off.'

The lady bridled. 'At fifteen pence a bottle? Not likely!'

'Use oranges instead,' I urged. 'This is doing you no good, and anyway oranges are easier to digest.'

She looked at me doubtfully. 'You wouldn't tell Dr Martin?'

'Of course I wouldn't. Let me empty this down the sink.'

Mrs Pringle sighed. 'Anything you say. I haven't got the strength to argue.'

She watched me as I approached the sink and unscrewed the bottle. The smell was certainly powerful. The liquid fizzed as it ran down the waste pipe.

'One thing,' she said, brightening, 'it'll clean out the drain lovely.'

It was certainly a pity that Mrs Pringle had not given the dining-room the attention it deserved, but I thought it looked quite grand enough to accommodate the managers.

There are six of them. The vicar is Chairman and has been for many years, and the next in length of service is the local farmer Mr Roberts.

When I first was appointed I was interviewed by Colonel Wesley and Miss Parr, both then nearing eighty, and now at rest in the neighbouring churchyard. Their places were taken by Mrs Lamb, the wife of the postmaster, and Peter Hale, a retired schoolmaster from Caxley, who is very highly regarded by the inhabitants of Fairacre and brings plenty of common sense and practical experience of schooling to the job.

The other two managers are Mrs Mawne and Mrs Moffat, the latter the sensible mother of Linda Moffat, the best dressed child in the school. She is particularly valuable, as she can put forward the point of view of parents generally, and is not too shy to speak her mind.

On Wednesday we had a full house, which is unusual. It is often Mr Roberts who is unable to be present and who sends a

message – or sometimes puts an apologetic face round the door – to say a ewe or cow is giving birth, or the harvest is at a crucial stage, and quite rightly we realize the necessity for putting first things first, and the meeting proceeds without him.

As well as the six managers Mr Salisbury arrived complete with pad for taking notes. I had a seat by him, with my usual brief report on such school matters as attendance, social activities and the like. Also in evidence were the log book of the school and the punishment book – the latter with its pages virtually unsullied since my advent.

The vicar made a polite little speech about the pleasure of using my house for the meeting. The minutes were read and signed and I gave my report.

There were the usual requests to the Office for more up-to-date lavatories and wash-basins. The skylight, which had defied generations of Fairacre's handy men to render it rainproof, was mentioned once more, and Mr Salisbury solemnly made notes on the pad. We fixed a date for our next term's meeting, and then settled back for Any Other Business.

'Is there any message, in particular,' asked Gerald Partridge, 'from the Office? We have heard some disquieting rumours.'

'Oh?' said Mr Salisbury. 'What about?'

'Might close the school,' said Mr Roberts, who does not mince words.

'*Really?*' cried Mrs Moffat. 'I hadn't heard a thing! Now that I get my groceries delivered I hardly ever go to the shop, and it's amazing how little one hears.'

'I've taken to going into Caxley for my provisions,' said Mrs Mawne conversationally. 'I can't say I enjoy these supermarkets, but when soap powder is ten pence cheaper it makes you think.'

'And bleaching liquid,' agreed Mrs Moffat, 'and things like tomato ketchup.'

'I make my own,' broke in Mrs Lamb. 'We grow more tomatoes than we can cope with, and it's no good trying to freeze them, and bottled tomatoes are not the same as fresh ones, are they? If you are interested, I've a very good recipe for ketchup I can let you have.'

The ladies accepted the offer enthusiastically. The vicar wore his resigned look. Most of our village meetings get out of hand like this, and he is quite used to waiting for these little asides to resolve themselves.

Mr Salisbury, tapping his expensive pen against his expensive false teeth, looked rather less patient, and cast meaningful glances at the Chairman.

Mrs Moffat had just embarked on a long and somewhat confused account about pickling walnuts when the vicar rapped gently on the table and said kindly: 'Order please, dear ladies, I think Mr Exeter has something to tell us.'

Mr Salisbury, taking his new name in his stride, put down the pad and assumed an expression of disarming candour.

'Well, I don't quite know just *what* you have been hearing at Fairacre, and I can assure you that the Office would always consult with the managers of any school as soon as the possibility of closure cropped up.'

'And has it?' asked Mr Roberts.

'There is always some chance of really small schools becoming uneconomic,' began Mr Salisbury cautiously.

He's been through this hoop many times before, I thought to myself. How far would he commit himself today?

'Fairacre's not really small,' said Mrs Mawne.

'I like a small school anyway,' pronounced Mrs Moffat.

'Much more friendly,' agreed Mrs Lamb.

'There are certain disadvantages,' said Mr Salisbury. 'Lack of team games, for instance. No specialist teachers on the staff for certain subjects. Older children get deprived.'

'*Deprived*?' squeaked Mrs Lamb. 'Our children aren't *deprived* are they, Miss Read?'

'I hope not,' I said.

'But what about Fairacre?' persisted Mr Roberts. 'Are you sharpening the knife for us?'

'Nothing will be done without your knowledge and cooperation,' repeated Mr Salisbury.

'But it's on the cards?' asked Peter Hale quietly. 'Is that it?'

'Numbers are going down steadily,' replied Mr Salisbury. 'We have to assess each case on its merit. Certainly, Fairacre is costing us a lot of money to maintain and the children might well be better off at a larger school.'

'Such as Beech Green?'

'Such as Beech Green,' agreed Mr Salisbury.

'When?' said Mr Roberts.

Mr Salisbury put down his pen and tilted back in his chair. I hoped that the rear legs of my elderly dining-room chair would stand the strain.

'It might be years. It all depends on numbers, on getting staff – a problem you are facing at the moment – and the feelings of managers and parents of the school.'

The vicar was looking unhappy. 'But what about Miss Read? It is unthinkable that she should have her school taken from her.'

There was a rumble of agreement round the table.

Mr Salisbury smiled at me. I felt like Red Riding Hood facing the wolf.

'Miss Read's welfare is our concern, of course. There would always be a post for her in the area. That I can promise you.'

'But we want her *here!*' wailed Mrs Lamb. 'And we *don't* want our school to close!'

'Absolutely right!' said Mrs Mawne. 'People in Fairacre simply won't stand for their children being uprooted, and carted away in buses like so many – er, so many—'

'Animals?' prompted Mr Roberts helpfully.

'No, no, not *animals*,' said Mrs Mawne testily. 'Animals don't go in buses! What I mean is, we won't have it. We'll never let Fairacre School close.' She looked round the table. Her face was red, her eyes bright. 'Agreed?'

'I do for one,' said Mr Roberts. 'I never heard such a shocking thing in my life. The idea of some of our little tots being hauled off to Beech Green fair gives me the shudders. This school's served the village for a hundred years, and I don't see why it shouldn't go on doing so for another hundred.'

'Hear! Hear!' said Mrs Lamb.

Mr Salisbury scribbled something on his pad, then looked up. 'Well, Mr Chairman, I have noted the objections of the managers, though I must point out that no decision of any kind has been taken by the committee about Fairacre School.'

'I hope nothing will ever happen to disturb the *status quo*,' said the vicar. 'We are all extremely happy with our little school. We should be deeply distressed if anything were done to close it, and we rely upon you to keep us informed of any developments.'

Mr Salisbury nodded agreement, and began to put his things together.

The vicar glanced at the clock. 'If that is all our business then nothing remains for me to do but to thank Mr Wells for coming here today and to remind you of the date of the next meeting.'

Mr Salisbury smiled at us all, shook my hand warmly and departed.

'He'd better not try any funny business with our village school,' said Mr Roberts, watching the car drive away. 'And don't you bother your head about all that nonsense, Miss Read. We're all behind you in this.'

'Indeed we are,' said the vicar.

'They closed Springbourne though,' said Mrs Moffat thoughtfully.

'Took 'em ten years,' observed Mr Roberts. 'A lot can happen before they think of Fairacre again. In any case, we can all have a damn good fight over it, and I bet we'd win. The parents would be with us, that I do know.'

One by one, the managers left, until only Mr Partridge remained with me.

'We don't seem to have gone very far with this business,' he remarked, 'but at least it has been mentioned, and I think that

is a good thing. He seems a good fellow, that Mr Wells –
Winchester, I mean—'

'Salisbury,' I interjected.

'*Salisbury* yes, *Salisbury*. I feel he would act honourably and
not do anything without letting us know first.'

'So I should hope.'

'Don't upset yourself about it, dear Miss Read. I cannot
believe that it would ever happen here.'

'Let's hope not,' I said. I really felt that I could not discuss
the wretched business any more, and I think the vicar sensed this,
for he patted my shoulder encouragingly, and made his departure.

I felt more shaken by the meeting than I would have admitted
to anyone. My mouth was dry, my knees wobbly. I tottered into
the garden and sat on the seat.

Everything around me burst with healthy life. Sparrows flashed
from plum tree to cherry tree. A peacock butterfly flapped its
bejewelled wings from a daisy top. The pinks gave out their heady
scent. The rose buds opened gently in the warm air. Even Tibby

displayed every sign of well-being, with her stomach exposed to the sun, and her eyes blissfully closed.

Only I, it seemed, was at odds with my surroundings. Their very beauty emphasized my own malaise. Should I ever come to terms with this horrible nagging uncertainty? Would it be better to take the bull by the horns, and apply for another post now? If I kept putting it off I should be too old to be considered by other managers. Perhaps I was too old already? How old was Emily Davis, I wondered, when she first heard that Springbourne was going to close? How long did Mr Roberts say that was hanging over her? Ten years? The suspense could not be borne.

At least, I told myself, no one need know yet about the shadow coming nearer. Enough to let the rumours die down, as they were doing quite comfortably, before stirring them up again like a swarm of angry bees.

I went indoors, at length, and tried to busy myself with bottling gooseberries, but the operation did not get my whole attention. I was glad when Mr Willet knocked at the back door and asked if he could borrow my edging shears.

It was a comfort to exchange a few general remarks with him on the state of our gardens, and the surprising need for rain at this time of year.

I accompanied him to the gate.

'All right if I bring these 'ere cutters back in the morning?' he asked.

'Fine,' I told him. 'I shan't be doing any gardening tonight.'

'I'd have an early night if I was you,' he advised me. 'You looks a bit peaky. I hears they brought up that school closing business again at your meeting. Bit of a shock, no doubt, but you put it out of your head.'

I was too stunned to reply.

He smiled kindly upon me. 'Us'll rout anyone who tries to shut up our school! You can bet your last farthing on that!'

He strode down the lane, my edging shears across his shoulder like a gun.

'There goes a militant Christian,' I said to Tibby, 'but how on earth did he know?'

7. TROUBLES NEVER COME SINGLY

Now that Amy had gone to attend to her other commitments, I was left to cope alone once again.

Luckily, it would be only for one week – or so the Office told me. After that, help was at hand in the form of Mrs Rose who had been headmistress of a small school near by. That school had been closed for some two years, and Mrs Rose was now euphoniously termed 'a peripatetic teacher'.

This meant that she moved from school to school, sometimes helping children who found reading difficult, and sometimes acting as a supply teacher when staff was short.

I viewed her advent with mixed feelings. She was over sixty, and was in this present job because she was in the last stages of her forty years' service. Her health was not good, and she was a martyr to laryngitis.

On the other hand, she was of a gentle disposition, anxious to fit in, open to suggestions, and generally amenable. And, in any case, the mere presence of another human being – even one as frail as Mrs Rose – on the other side of the glass partition, was a great comfort and support.

In the meantime, I soldiered on and was relieved, in a way, to have the school to myself in order to try to come to terms with the dreadful possibility of becoming, like Mrs Rose, a teacher without a school of my own.

Despite my airy dismissal of rumours on so many earlier occasions, this time I had an uncomfortable feeling that change was in the wind. Something in Mr Salisbury's manner at the managers' meeting made me fear the worst, and I was surprised to find how upset I was.

Normally, I slept for nine hours, drugged with work and good downland air. Now I took an hour or more before drifting off, as I tossed and turned trying to decide what to do. Even my appetite suffered, a most unusual symptom, and I found myself nibbling a biscuit with cheese rather than facing a square meal in the evening. What Amy would have said if she could have witnessed my more than usually casual eating habits, I shuddered to think.

Now and again, I found myself trembling too. Good heavens, was I becoming senile into the bargain? Fat chance I should have of landing another teaching post if I appeared before strange managers with my head shaking and possibly a drop on the end of my nose!

It was all extremely unnerving, and I was grateful for the children's company in my alarming condition.

There were other disquieting factors. The weather had turned cold and blustery, despite the fact that June had arrived. We could have done with some heating from the tortoise stoves, but that, of course, was out of the question.

Then Minnie Pringle's presence about the house on Friday afternoons was distinctly unsettling. On the first visit, she had managed to drop a jar of bath salts into the hand basin, smashing the former and badly cracking the latter.

Also, in a fit of zeal, she had attacked my frying pan with disinfectant powder kept for the dustbin, and some steel wool, thus effectively removing the non-stick surface.

'I thought as it was Vim,' she explained, in answer to my questioning.

'But it says DISINFECTANT POWDER on the tin!'

'Can't read them long words,' said Minnie truculently.

'But you can read "Vim", can't you? And this tin didn't have "Vim" written on it.'

'Looked the same to me,' replied Minnie, and flounced off,

tripping over a rug on the way, and bringing the fire-irons into the hearth with a fearful crash.

I fled into the garden, unable to face any more destruction. So must victims of earthquakes feel, I thought, as they await the next shattering blow.

It was during this unsettled period that the case of Arthur Coggs and his companions was heard at Caxley.

As they appeared in Court on market day, several people from Fairacre were interested spectators, among them Mr Willet. He had travelled in by bus to pick up some plants from the market, and having two hours to spare before the bus returned, decided to witness the fate of the four accused.

Mr Lovejoy, the most respected solicitor in Caxley, was defending all four, as he had done on many previous occasions.

'And an uphill job he'll have this time,' commented Mr Willet to me. 'They had the sauce to plead Not Guilty, too.'

'Perhaps it's true,' I said.

Mr Willet snorted, puffing out his stained moustache. 'Want to bet on it? Anyway, old Colonel Austin was in the chair, and he read out a bit, before they got started, about committing 'em to Crown Court if they was found guilty. Something about their characters and antecedents, whatever that means. But it made it plain that they could get clobbered for more than six months, if need be, and I'd stake my oath that's where they'll end up. All four's got a list as long as my arm, as everyone knows.'

'A man is innocent,' I said primly, 'until he is proved guilty.'

'Them four,' replied Mr Willet, 'are as innocent as Old Nick hisself. My heart bleeds for that chap Lovejoy trying to white-wash them villains. It'd turn my stomach to do a job like that. I'd sooner dig Hundred Acre Field with a hand fork, that I would!'

On Monday morning, Mrs Rose arrived in good time, in a little car, shabby and battered enough to win approval from Mrs Pringle, in whose eyes it appeared a very suitable form of transport for teachers. Amy's large high-powered beauty had always offended Mrs Pringle's sense of fitness. She opened the gates for Mrs Rose's vehicle with never a trace of a limp, or a word of complaint. Clearly, Mrs Rose was accepted, and that was a great relief to me.

She looked frailer than ever, and also decidedly chilly in a sleeveless cotton frock.

'I'd no idea it would be so cold,' she said, clutching her goose-fleshed arms. 'It is *June*, after all!'

'It's always colder up here on the downs,' I told her, 'and these old buildings are pretty damp. We grow quite a good crop of toadstools in the map cupboard when the weather's right.'

She was not amused. I hastily changed my tactics.

'Come over to the house,' I urged, 'and we'll find you a cardigan. It will be too big, I fear, but at least you will be warm.'

Tibby greeted us effusively, no doubt imagining that the

morning session had gone by with unprecedented speed, and it was now time for a mid-day snack.

Mrs Rose paused to take in my accommodation and furnishings before coming upstairs with me.

'I used to have a nice little house like this,' she mourned.

I felt very sorry for her, and slightly guilty too. I certainly was lucky, that I knew. All the old fears of losing my home came fluttering back as we mounted the stairs. I did my best to fight them off.

I set out a selection of woollen garments, and she chose a thick Shetland wool cardigan which would have kept out an arctic wind. It would certainly mitigate the chill of Fairacre School in June.

Her eyes wandered over the bedroom as she did up the buttons.

'You have made it so pretty and snug,' she said enviously. 'I had much the same curtains when I was in the school house at Bedworth.'

'I always admired the garden when I passed that way,' I said hastily, trying to wean her from her nostalgia. 'The roses always seemed so fine in that part of the country. Clay soil, I suppose. What sort of garden do you have now in Caxley?'

I could not have done worse.

'I've no garden at all! Just a window box in my upstairs flat. I can't tell you how much I miss everything.'

The sound of infants screaming in the playground saved me from commenting.

'I think we'd better go back,' I said, leading the way downstairs, 'or we may find spilt blood.'

But all was comparatively calm, and I led Mrs Rose inside to show her the infants' room, and to introduce her to Mrs Pringle.

That lady was leaning against the doorway, upturned broom in hand, looking rather like Britannia with her trident, but a good deal less comely. She bowed her head graciously to Mrs Rose.

'We met at Mrs Denham's auction sale,' she reminded the new teacher. 'I remember it well because you bid against me for a chest of drawers.'

Mrs Rose looked nervous.

'Not that you missed much,' continued Mrs Pringle. 'Even though it was knocked down to me at four pounds. The bottom drawer jams something cruel, and them handles pulls of in your hand. We've had to glue 'em in time and time again.'

I thought, once again, on hearing this snippet of past history, that life in a small community is considerably brightened by such memories as this one of a shared occasion. Some of these joltings of memory are caused by pure happiness – others, as in this present case, owe their sharpness to a certain tartness in the situation. Obviously, Mrs Pringle's bad bargain had caused some rankling since the day of the ladies' battle for the chest of drawers.

'Miss!' shouted Ernest, appearing on the scene. 'Can I ring the bell, miss? Can I? Can I ring the bell?'

'Yes, yes,' I replied. 'And there's no need to rush in here as though a bull were after you.'

I ushered Mrs Rose into the infants' room as the bell clanged out its message to my tardy school children still in the fields and lanes of Fairacre.

The *Caxley Chronicle* carried a full report of Arthur Coggs' case that week, and eagerly devoured it was by all his neighbours in Fairacre. There is nothing so comforting as reading about others' tribulations. It reminds one of one's own good fortune.

The prosecution's most weighty piece of evidence, in more senses than one, was the entire piece of lead roofing which was carried into Court by six sweating policemen.

A plan was handed up to the Bench, and the magistrates were invited to compare the shape of the roof displayed on the paper before them, with that of the lead, now being unrolled and stamped into place beneath large feet, on the floor below.

After old Miss Dewbury's plan had been put the right way up for her by a kindly fellow-justice, the magistrates gave their attention to the matter with more than usual liveliness.

Amazing how they come to life, thought Mr Lovejoy, when a few pictures or objects to play with are handed up! Glazing eyes sparkled, sagging shoulders were braced. Could it be that addresses given by prosecution and defence sometimes bored the Bench? Not, thought Mr Lovejoy seriously, when he addressed them. He had a turn of phrase, he fancied, which commanded respect as well as attention to his cause, but possibly some of his learned colleagues were less fortunate in their powers. (Mr Lovejoy, it will be noted, was without humour.)

Certainly, there was a surprising likeness between the plan and the cumbersome evidence on the floor. The lead undoubtedly came from a small building with an octagonal roof like Mr Mawne's. It had been found, the magistrates were told, hidden under a pile of sacks in the Bryant brothers' outhouse. They looked suitably impressed.

Mr Lovejoy, on the other hand, looked calm and faintly disdainful. His eye fixed on the pitch-pine ceiling of the Victorian court house, he was clearly rehearsing his speech which would show that a person or persons unknown had humped the lead, from a source equally unknown, and dumped it upon the Bryants' premises with the intention of getting them into their present unfortunate position.

The case ground on for the rest of the morning, and continued after the lunch break. Witnesses were called by the indefatigable Mr Lovejoy, who testified to the fact that the accused had been in their company, regularly each evening, whilst imbibing, in a modest fashion, as befitted their unemployed state, at local hostelries.

At four o'clock Miss Dewbury was nudged into wakefulness, the accused men were told that the charge against them had been proved, and the prosecutor handed up long lists of previous convictions for the Bench to study.

The Chairman, Colonel Austin, after a brief word with his colleagues, then committed them in custody to the Crown Court for sentence, just as Mr Willet had prophesied, and they left the Court escorted by two policemen.

Mr Lovejoy shuffled his papers together, bowed politely, and hurried after his clients.

'That is the business of the Court,' announced the clerk, 'and the business of the day is over.'

'And only just in time,' observed old Miss Dewbury as she departed. 'I put a beef casserole in the oven at lunch time, and it must be nearly dry by now.'

'Never like sending chaps to prison,' grunted Colonel Austin to his male colleague, as they reached for their hats, 'but what can you do with four like that? How many times have we seen 'em, John?'

'Too many,' replied his friend, 'and we'll see them again the minute they're out!'

In Fairacre, reaction to the Court's decision was mixed. Most agreed that Arthur Coggs was only getting his just deserts, and speculated upon how long the Judge would give all four when the time came. But more were concerned about the effect of Arthur's absence on his wife and family.

'She'll be a damn sight better off without him around,' said Mr Willet. 'What good's he to her, poor soul? She'll get the social security money to herself now, instead of watching Arthur swilling it down his throat at the Beetle. Besides, she won't get knocked about. Make a nice change for her, I'd say, to have a peaceful house for a time.'

To my surprise, Mrs Pringle took another view.

'She'll miss him, I'll be bound, bad lot though he is. A woman needs a man's company about the house.'

'I can't say I've missed it,' I observed. 'And I could well do without Arthur Coggs' company, at any time.'

'Yes, well,' admitted Mrs Pringle, 'there's some as lead an *unnatural* life, so their opinions don't altogether matter.'

'Thank you,' I said. My sarcasm was ignored, as Mrs Pringle followed her train of thought.

'I knows he keeps her short of money. I know he raises his hand to her—'

'And his boot,' put in Mr Willet.

'And I knows his language is plain 'orrible when he's in liquor, but then she's used to it, and used to having him around the place. She'll be terrible lonely with him gone.'

Several other people echoed Mrs Pringle's comments, but the general feeling was that Mrs Coggs must be relieved she was safe from physical assault, at least for a year or more. A number of inhabitants went even further in their concern, among them Gerald Partridge the vicar, who spoke about the family to me.

'I am right in thinking that the Coggs children get free dinners?'

I reassured him on this point.

'And their clothing? Shoes and so on. Are they adequately provided for? I should be only too happy to give something, you know, if it could be done without causing distress to poor Mrs Coggs. She has enough to bear as it is.'

I said that I tried to keep an eye on that side of things, and had been lucky enough to get Mrs Moffat and other generous parents to hand down garments that were little worn directly to Mrs Coggs, instead of sending them, in the usual way, to our local jumble sales.

'She won't be too badly off,' I promised him. I could not bear to see his gentle face puckered with anxiety. 'And now Arthur is out of the way, I believe she will take on more work.'

'Yes, indeed. Mrs Mawne is having her there for a morning. I gather that Minnie Pringle insisted on dusting some very precious glass cases housing some of Mr Mawne's rarer birds, and two were broken, most unfortunately. Mr Mawne was a little put out about it, and fired the girl on the spot.'

Later I was to hear from Minnie's own lips, the exact words used by her irate employer – short, brutal, words of Anglo-

Saxon origin – which, I felt, had been put to their proper use under the circumstances.

'Well, I'm glad to know Mrs Coggs has got the job,' I said. 'It will give her an added interest as well as more money. But don't worry too much about her. The social security office will see she is looked after, and really she's so much better off without that ghastly husband.'

The vicar looked shocked. 'Strong words, Miss Read, strong words! He is one of my flock, remember, even if he has strayed, and I can only hope that his present afflictions will make him change his ways.'

'That'll be the day,' I said.

But I said it when the vicar had departed.

PART TWO

Fairacre Hears the News

* * *

8. A Welcome Diversion

One summer afternoon, soon after the vicar's visit, I had a surprise call from Amy and Vanessa.

The children had just run home, glad to be out in the sunshine, and I was just about to make tea.

Vanessa, a niece of James, Amy's husband, was always attractive, but now, in pregnancy, had that added lustre of skin and hair which so often goes with the condition. I said, truthfully, how radiant she looked.

'But *enormous*!' protested Vanessa, holding out her arms sideways, the better to display her bulging form. 'I'd no idea one could stretch to this size. All those women's magazines chat away about letting out skirts a few inches, as time goes by! My dear, *look* at me! This is a shirt which was too big for Tarquin, who stands six feet four as you know, and even this is getting tight. I'm thinking of hiring a bell tent.'

'A dirndl skirt's the answer,' said Amy, 'with a huge smock over it. Or a kaftan, perhaps.' She gazed at Vanessa with a thoughtful smile. 'There's no denying that one really does need a waist for most clothes.'

'Well, I hope to have one again in a few weeks' time,' replied Vanessa, settling her bulk on the sofa.

'Put your feet up,' I urged.

'Too much effort, darling. I really don't recommend this baby business. Don't attempt it.'

'I should get the sack if I did,' I told her.

'Which reminds me,' said Amy, 'what news of Fairacre School closing?'

75

I felt Amy could have been a little more tactful, but forbore to comment upon it.

'Not much, but something's in the wind. George Annett has been asked to send in lists of equipment he would need if another class were added to his school – or possibly two classes.'

'It does sound ominous.'

'It does indeed. But there's mighty little one can do until I hear something more definite. It seems silly to try for another post when I'm so settled here, and in any case, all this may come to nothing.'

Amy fixed a steady gaze upon me. 'Poor old dear,' she said, so sympathetically that I was glad to turn away from her and busy myself with pouring tea.

'Vanessa is staying for a whole week,' she went on, 'and I wondered if you would come over for dinner one evening?'

'You know I'd love to,' I said, carrying a cup to the recumbent figure on the sofa. Vanessa struggled to a more upright position.

'I'll just lodge it on this bulge,' she said with a dazzling smile. 'It really comes in quite useful, this extra shelf. I shall miss it. Sometimes I think I shall give birth to at least *three* babies.'

'Don't the doctors know?'

'My own, who is a sweetie, says twins. The other chap, a top-flight gynaecologist, won't commit himself, but then he's terribly cautious. Always worrying about his hypocrites' oath, I think.'

'*Hippocrates*, Vanessa!' exclaimed Amy. 'Really, when I think of the money spent on your education and see the result, I shudder!'

'I have a cosy little argument with him sometimes,' continued Vanessa unabashed, 'just to stretch his mind, you know. "If I had a tumour on the brain, which meant I was a living vegetable, don't you think you should put me gently to sleep?" I ask him. Of course, he gets in a terrible fluster, and talks about this old hypocrites' oath he took when he was a beardless boy, and we both thoroughly enjoy a little abstract thinking after all the dreadfully coarse back-and-forth about bowels and heartburn.'

Vanessa sighed, and the teacup wobbled dangerously.

'I must say it will be quite a relief to know how many. Luckily, I've been given enough baby clothes for a dozen. Tarquin's mother is a great knitter, and does everything in half-dozens. Even *binders*! I don't think babies have them now, but I haven't the heart to tell her. She's also presented me with a dozen long flannel things, all exquisitely feather-stitched, which have to be pinned over the baby's feet to keep it warm. I can't see the monthly nurse using those.'

'You're having it at home then?' I said.

'Good heavens, yes! All the family's babies have to be born in the castle, and the piper waits outside – for days sometimes – ready to play the bagpipes to welcome the child.'

'I'd have a relapse,' I said. 'To my Sassenach ear "The Flowers of the Forest" sounds exactly like "The Keel Row".'

'Well, don't let Tarquin know,' advised Vanessa. 'The sound of the bagpipes brings tears to his eyes.'

'He's not the only one,' I told her, rescuing her empty cup.

On the Saturday following Amy's visit, I was invited to attend a lecture by Henry Mawne. It was to be held in the Corn Exchange in Caxley, and the subject was 'European Birds of Prey', illustrated by slides taken by the speaker.

I was a little surprised by the invitation. The Mawnes are always very kind to me, but we do not meet a great deal, except by chance, in the village. The vicar and Mrs Partridge were also going, and several other people from Fairacre.

All had been invited to lunch with the Mawnes at the Buttery, a restaurant in Caxley, conveniently placed near the hall, and offering a varied menu at modest prices. The Buttery is always busy, and many a local reputation has been shredded beneath its oak beams.

If I had been rather more alert when Mrs Mawne invited me I might have excused myself, for Saturday afternoons are usually taken up with household chores, cooking, mending, or entertaining, which get left undone during the week. But as usual, I was not prepared, and found myself at twelve o'clock on the Saturday in question, trying to decide between a long-sleeved silk frock (too dressy?) or a pink linen suit, rather too tight in the skirt, which Amy had kindly told me made me look like mutton dressed as lamb.

I decided on the latter.

There were four cars going from Fairacre, and I went with Diana and Peter Hale.

'Wonder how long this affair will last?' mused Peter Hale. 'I want to drop in at school to see some of the cricket. Diana will drive you home. I'm getting a lift with the new classics man. He passes the house.'

'I think, you know,' said Diana gently, 'that Henry Mawne is afraid that the Corn Exchange is going to be far too big for this afternoon's lecture. I hear that he suggested that a party from Beech Green might help to swell the ranks.'

Light began to dawn.

'He'll need several hundreds to make a good sprinkling in that barn of a place,' I said. 'Why not find something smaller?'

'Everything was booked up,' said Peter, jamming on his brakes as a pheasant strolled haughtily across the road. 'Half the jumble sales and bazaars seem to take place on Saturdays. I can't think why.'

'Most people have been paid on Friday,' I told him. 'It's as simple as that.'

We had the usual trundling round Caxley to find a place to leave the car, and were lucky enough to snap up the last place in a car park fairly near the restaurant. Secretly, I was glad. It was not the pink skirt alone that was tight. My new shoes were killing me. Could I be growing a corn on my little toe? And if so, would I need to go to a chiropodist? What a terrible thought! Hopelessly ticklish, I should be hysterical if my feet were handled, and what if she – or he, perhaps? – wanted to file my toe-nails? That could not be borne.

A prey to these fears, I hobbled in the wake of the Hales and entered the bustle and heat of the Buttery.

The Mawnes greeted us cheerfully, and we were seated at the Buttery's largest table. It was clear that we should be about a dozen in all, and the manager had done us proud with six pink carnations in a hideous glass vase with coloured knobs on it.

Margaret and Mary Waters, two spinster sisters who share a cottage in Fairacre, arrived, with the vicar and Mrs Partridge, and four more friends of the Mawnes made up the party.

Menus were handed round, and we studied them seriously. For most of us it was a pleasure to have a choice of dishes. After all, I was usually grateful, at this time of day, for a plain school dinner. To be offered such attractions as melon, prawn cocktail, pâté or soup – for first course alone – was wholly delightful, and I began to enjoy myself enormously.

Our host did not appear to be so happy. I remembered that his wife had once told me that he dreaded any sort of public speaking, and was a prey to nerves before these events.

'What is this blanket of veal?' he was asking her crossly.

'You won't like it. It's veal in white sauce.'

'How disgusting! *Blanket*'s just about the right word for it.' He turned to the vicar. 'Don't you hate white gravy, padre? It's like cold soup – dead against nature.'

'I must admit,' replied Gerald Partridge, 'that I rather like things in white sauce. So bland, you know. Take tripe, for instance—'

'No, *you* take tripe,' exclaimed Henry, shuddering, 'I never could face that awfully rubbery flannel look, let alone put it in my mouth.'

'Done with onions,' said Margaret Waters earnestly, 'it can be quite delicious. And so nourishing. My poor father practically lived on it for the last few weeks of his life.'

Peter Hale caught my eye across the table, and I had to concentrate on the carnations to preserve my sobriety.

'I should have the lamb chops, Henry,' said Mrs Mawne

decisively. 'I see there are new potatoes and peas, and you know you always enjoy them.'

Henry brightened a little.

'But what about our guests? Come now, Miss Read, what are you having?'

I said I should like melon, and then, bravely, the *blanquette de veau*.

The waiter, who had been leaning against a nearby dresser looking bored to distraction, now deigned to approach and started to take down orders.

As always, the meal was good. Caxley people are fond of their food, and are quite ready to complain if it is not to their liking. The Buttery knows its customers, and does its best to give satisfaction.

By the time the cheese board was going the rounds we were all in fine spirits, except for poor Henry Mawne who was becoming more agitated as the dreaded hour drew near.

'I've forgotten my reading glasses,' he exclaimed fretfully, slapping each pocket in turn. 'Now what do I do?'

Mrs Mawne remained calm. 'You use your bifocals, as you always do, Henry. Really, *the fuss*!'

'You know I never feel right with bifocals at a lecture,' wailed Henry, for all the world like one of my eight-year-olds.

Gerald Partridge leant forward anxiously. 'Shall I get the car, and go back for them?' he offered. 'I could be back here in half an hour.'

Mrs Mawne took charge. 'Certainly not, Gerald. I won't hear of it! You are the soul of kindness, but there is absolutely *no need* for Henry to have his reading glasses. And well he knows it!'

She looked severely at her husband, who seeing himself beaten, turned his attention to a splendid Stilton cheese clothed in a snowy napkin, and began to look less fractious.

His guests became more relaxed, and the conversation turned to Arthur Coggs and his future.

'A friend of mine,' said Mary Waters, 'was in court when

they carried in that massive piece of lead. Poor Albert Phipps nearly had a rapture!'

'A careless one?' inquired Peter Hale.

'You mean a *rupture*, dear,' said her sister reprovingly. 'You always get that word wrong. A *rapture*, as Mr Hale has reminded us, is what dear Ivor Novello wrote about.'

'I'm sorry,' said Peter, 'I was being flippant.'

'My English teacher once said: "Flippancy gets you nowhere,"' remarked his wife. 'I'd been trying to show off, I remember, about "trembling ears" in Milton. I said that the phrase smacked of the asinine, and was ticked off, quite rightly. Schoolgirls must be very trying to teach.'

'No worse than schoolboys,' commented Henry.

'I agree with that wholeheartedly,' said Peter Hale, schoolmaster.

Someone then looked at the clock and murmured that perhaps we should be moving. Henry Mawne's agitation returned.

'The bill, waiter! Quickly, my dear fellow. We mustn't be late.'

The waiter ambled off at a leisurely pace, while we collected bags and gloves and various other impedimenta, and Henry Mawne started his pocket-slapping again in the frenzy of finding his cheque book.

'Henry,' said his wife, with a look which could have stopped a rogue elephant in its tracks. 'Calm down! You know perfectly well that I have the cheque book in my handbag. Now, if you will make sure that you have your notes and your bifocals, I will take charge of the account and meet you outside.'

We gave our sincere thanks to the Mawnes for the delicious lunch as we made our way to the Corn Exchange. The Caxley market square was gay with stalls, and I should dearly have loved to buy some eggs and cheese from my favourite stallholder, but this was not the time, I realized, to clutch a piece of ripe gorgonzola for an hour and a half.

The hall was half full, which was a creditable number to assemble on a Saturday afternoon. As we were the speaker's party, we were shown to the front row. On the way to our august places, I was delighted to catch sight of a contingent from Beech Green. Among the party I saw George and Isabel Annett and dear Miss Clare, who taught for many years at Fairacre School, sitting with them.

I was seated by Mrs Mawne, who remained completely unmoved by the pathetic sight of her husband trying to arrange his papers with shaking hands.

The chairman was the president of Caxley's Nature Conservancy Trust and was doing his best to put Henry at his ease before starting the meeting. He might just as well have saved his breath, for Henry took not the slightest notice, and brought matters to a climax by dropping all his papers on the floor.

With startled cries the two men bent to retrieve them, cracking their skulls together, thus occasioning further cries from the audience. The papers were collected, Henry shuffled them together with a look of utter despair, and the chairman rose to introduce him.

Once Henry was on his feet, and the clapping had died away,

he became wonderfully calm and happy. He smiled at us all, as though he were truly glad to tell us about the birds which gave such zest and joy to his life. It was difficult to believe that less than half an hour ago, he had been as nervous as a fretful baby.

It was an enthralling talk, and the slides were superb. When he ended, the audience applauded enthusiastically. Clearly, here was a man who was master of his subject and able to transmit his own excitement to others.

As we drove home, Diana Hale summed up the feelings of us all.

'He's a man who can make you forget your own world, and carry you into his.'

With a start, I realized how true this was.

For the first time for weeks, I had forgotten the shadow which hung menacingly over my future, and gratitude mingled with admiration for our old friend Henry Mawne.

9 · Mrs Pringle Goes to War

Minnie Pringle continued to wreak havoc in my house every Friday afternoon. I did my best to forestall trouble, but was far from successful.

Now that I realized that she could not read, I tried to put out the bottles and tins she would need for any specific job. Sometimes it worked. Sometimes such bottles as that containing window-cleaning liquid would be put in the bathroom cabinet beside witch hazel or gargle. It was all a little unnerving.

My vacuum cleaner was maltreated weekly by having its cord twisted tightly into figures of eight round the handle, and the plug became so cracked with being dropped on the tiled floor of the kitchen, that I was obliged to renew it. Maddening though she was, I did not want to find Minnie electrocuted on my premises.

She also had a peculiar way with dusters. Somewhere along the extensive line of previous employers, she had picked up the wholly admirable habit of washing the dusters before leaving work.

Unfortunately, how to dry them seemed to be beyond her. I had indicated a small line conveniently near to the back door, but this was ignored. Sometimes she hung a wet duster on the newel post at the foot of the stairs, so that anyone mounting clapped her hand upon the clammy object. When remonstrated with, Minnie changed her tactics and draped them along the newly polished dining-room table, or over the padded back of an armchair.

Irritation gave way to incredulity, and I used to return to my home on Friday afternoons wondering what Minnie had got up to this time. There was always something untoward to greet me. If there were not some new places for the dusters to dry, then it might be a few broken shards of a favourite cup, carefully arranged on a half-sheet of newspaper on the draining board. At least, she did not try to cover up her little mishaps with my property. I supposed it was something to be thankful for, but I longed for the day when Minnie's future took her far, far away.

Her own domestic affairs seemed to be shrouded in mystery. I had heard rumours about Mrs Fowler and her new paramour, and some said that she was asserting her authority to such an extent that it was likely that Minnie's husband might return to his wife and children. Others said that Minnie too was finding consolation elsewhere, and that the under-gardener at Springbourne Manor had been seen leaving Minnie's premises at some very odd times.

I rarely saw Minnie, only the results of her labours, and that was quite enough for me. Mrs Pringle, who usually volunteered any village news, was unusually taciturn these days, and I put it down to the debilitating effects of the diet. Not that she seemed any thinner, but she was certainly paler, and her limp seemed to be permanent these days.

I ventured to ask how the dieting was progressing one day.

'You wants to ask Dr Martin,' she said sourly. 'It's him what does the worrying. I told him straight: "Them scales of yourn are wrong," but he never batted an eyelid. He reckons I've only lost another two pound, after all this time. Not my fault, you know, I sticks to what's writ down.'

It did seem odd.

'Of course, I eats what's put afore me if I'm invited out. Stands to reason you can't offend people when they've slaved over a hot stove getting a nice bit of roast pork and potatoes ready, and a good suet pudden to follow.'

'But do you go out often?'

'Twice a week to my sister's. And of course I have her back, and have to do much the same for her.'

'That can't help,' I felt obliged to point out.

Mrs Pringle bridled. 'I've halved my chocolate! I'm used to what we knew as a tuppeny bar in the old days, after my tea. Well, I makes that do for two days now, and I only takes one spoonful of sugar instead of two in my tea. No call for Dr Martin to be so sharp with me, I tell him. After all, I'm still *losing* weight, aren't I?'

I began to feel sorry for Dr Martin.

'Couldn't you use those sweeteners instead of sugar, and perhaps have half an apple instead of the chocolate?'

Mrs Pringle looked at me as if I were an earwig discovered in the bedclothes.

'And start my heart-burn up again? It's plain to see, Miss Read, as you and Dr Martin is hand in glove. If you wants me to go on working here, day in and day out, giving of my best and my heart's blood to this 'ere thankless job, then I must have a bit of nourishing food.'

She made her way towards the door, limping heavily.

I said no more. I know when I am beaten.

The second half of the Summer term brought some of the hottest weather of the century. Day after day dawned clear and cloudless, and by half past ten in the morning, it was beginning to get too hot for comfort outside.

Our ancient schoolroom was one of the coolest places in the village. With its lofty ceiling and high windows, it was remarkably airy, and the gnarled elder trees which tapped against the west-facing windows, cast a green shade which was more than welcome.

The door was propped open permanently to let in any stray breeze. It also let in Tibby, much to the rapture of the children, and an assortment of wild life ranging from wasps – which threw the children into violent demonstrations of assumed fear – to butterflies and, once, a fieldmouse.

The latter threw *me* into a transport of fear, which was certainly not assumed, but which I tried to hide from the children. My efforts were not completely successful.

'Shall I whack it on the 'ead?' inquired Ernest, advancing with his geography reader in hand.

'No, no,' I said hastily. After all my exhortations on kindness to animals, it was disappointing to see Ernest's blood-thirsty reaction to the intruder. 'It will find its way out in a minute.'

Nose twitching, it scampered along by the map cupboard, watched by the class. I observed its movements with inward horror. Suppose it turned in my direction?

As luck would have it, Patrick gave an enormous sneeze, which sent it bolting from the room, and out once again to the field from which it had emerged.

I breathed again.

The afternoons were so hot that it was impossible to expect much in the way of work from the children. The older ones went by school bus to Caxley once a week for a swimming lesson, and were the envy of all those left behind to swelter in the heat of Fairacre.

I did my best to make their lot easier by taking them outside. We have one particularly fine beech tree near the edge of the field which borders the playground, and here the shade was deep and refreshing on those baking afternoons.

I read them folk tales, and let them lie as they pleased, flat on their backs, or lodged on an elbow, their hair lifting in the light wind that stirred the leaves above them. What did it matter if they heard little of the story? On those golden afternoons they absorbed more than any printed page could give them – happy summer memories which would remain with them for a life-time.

Whether it was the heat, or Mrs Pringle's growing touchiness, or a combination of both, which triggered off the great row between that lady and inoffensive Mrs Rose, it is impossible to say.

It began one hot after-dinner session, and the battleground was the lobby at the back of the school where Mrs Pringle does the washing-up.

It is usually a peaceful period, preceding the afternoon session, and occasionally running into the first lesson. I am quite used to giving out handiwork material to the background of clashing cutlery and Mrs Pringle's contralto rendering of the more lugubrious numbers from *Hymns Ancient and Modern*.

The first I heard was the sound of infants on the move next door. They were obviously surging towards the door leading into the lobby. Adult voices were raised, one shrill, one booming. The latter was only too familiar to me, but I could not think who the other shrill-voiced contestant could be.

Daring my children to bat an eyelid, I strode forth to investigate.

'Into your seats this minute!' I bellowed at Mrs Rose's excited children, who were milling round the door. Reluctantly they obeyed, and I posted the largest infant at the front to tell me on my return who had been the quietest. The battle was gaining in volume and speed of action behind me.

It was now plain that Mrs Rose was engaged in combat with Mrs Pringle, and I quaked at the thought of what I might see by – or even under – the lobby sink.

There was something Wagnerian about the sight which met my eyes. Steam from the washing-up bowl wreathed the forms of the two martial bodies. Mrs Pringle held a saucepan aloft as though about to cleave Mrs Rose's skull, some inches below her own. Mrs Rose, her normally pale face suffused with blotchy red patches, clung to Mrs Pringle's flowered overall and screamed her head off.

'*Ladies!*' I shouted. It seemed a singularly inappropriate title to bestow upon the two viragos before me, but was the best I could manage. At least it had the desired effect, and the combatants parted and faced me, bosoms heaving and eyes flashing. They were too winded with warfare to speak.

'What on *earth*,' I said sternly, 'are you two doing? You are frightening the life out of the children.'

This was not strictly true. Even now, some bold bad infants had crept to the doorway and were surveying the scene with every appearance of joy. This little contretemps would soon be common knowledge in Fairacre, I surmised.

'Go back,' I hissed, 'into your seats this instant! The very idea!'

This last phrase, idiotic though it may be, has an uncanny power over the young, if expressed forcibly. It worked yet again, and the faces vanished.

Mrs Rose tidied her hair, and without a word, followed her pupils, leaving Mrs Pringle muttering malevolently to herself.

'I don't know what all that was about, and I don't *want* to know,' I said loftily, 'but if it happens again we shall have to look for another cleaner.'

'And lucky you'll be to get one with that old cat on the premises,' boomed Mrs Pringle, as I departed with as much dignity as I could muster.

Mrs Rose was tying a shoelace with trembling fingers, as I passed through the infants' room on the way to my own.

'Sorry about that,' she whispered. 'I'll tell you all at play-time.'

A rare silence had fallen upon her class. They gazed upon her round-eyed. I left her to face the infants alone. My own children were equally silent, but their eyes were bright with expectation.

'See if you can stay as quiet as that for the next ten minutes,' I said frostily, propping myself on the edge of the table, and trying to regain composure.

Long-suffering looks were exchanged. Obviously not a word of explanation was going to be given them. Was there no justice?

I saw Mrs Pringle departing soon afterwards, her black bag swinging on her arm, her stout back registering martyrdom, and her limp much in evidence.

Mrs Rose, calmer now, told me about the cause of the fuss, as we sipped our tea in the playground.

The real culprits were some new infants who had emptied their dinner scraps into the wrong bucket. It was as simple as that.

From time immemorial, Mrs Pringle has taken home a dank parcel of plate-scrapings for her chickens. This is one of the many uses to which her black oilcloth bag is pressed. One bucket stands beneath the sink for such revolting left-overs as fat-trimmings, tough morsels of cabbage stalk and so on, combined with gobbets of custard, jelly or pastry from the second course.

Sometimes, turning from this receptacle with nausea, I am reminded of the tubs which are reputed to have been left outside the gates of Blenheim Palace, years ago, for the poor of Woodstock. It took an American Duchess to suggest that at least the savoury matter could be put in a separate container from the sweet. Mrs Pringle's chickens are not so fortunate, but appear to thrive on what they get.

The second bucket contains the true rubbish destined for the dustbin, along with the contents of the wastepaper baskets. What had happened was that four or five innocents had scraped their plates into the latter, and such delicacies as half chewed gristle, dear to the hearts of Mrs Pringle's hens, were in danger of being thrown out.

Nagged by pain from her empty stomach, Mrs Pringle reacted furiously to this scandalous filching from her hungry hens, and began berating the poor infants who soon began to weep.

Mrs Rose, as zealous for her children as Mrs Pringle was for her chickens, rushed to their defence, and the ugly scene then ensued.

'She had no business to shout at the children like that,' asserted Mrs Rose, pink at the memory. 'Nor at me. I've never in my life been subjected to such impertinence.'

'I think you could have been a little more tolerant,' I said mildly. 'You know what Mrs Pringle is – and since this confounded dieting she's been twice as touchy.'

'She's not going to yell at my babies and get away with it! I shall expect an apology!'

'You won't get it.'

And of course she didn't. Mrs Pringle wrapped herself in majestic silence, and so did Mrs Rose, so that the atmosphere fairly quivered with taut nerves whenever the two ladies were in the same room.

It was a trying time for us all, and the fact that nothing more had beeen said, one way or the other, about Fairacre School's possible closure, I found particularly unnerving. More measuring had been going on at Beech Green School, according to Mr Annett, but otherwise he too was in the dark.

'I think it will all blow over,' he told me one sunny Friday evening. He had called before choir practice to lend me an

American treatise on educating young children which he thought I might enjoy.

I had not the heart to tell him that any book more than three inches thick, with footnotes and five appendices, killed any desire to read it, from the start. A quick look inside had confirmed my suspicions that this one had been written in the brain-numbing sort of jargon I cannot abide. There was no doubt about it. It was one of those books one keeps safely for a decent interval, dusts, and returns, praying that the lender refrains from asking questions on it.

'After all,' he continued, 'it always has before. Why should they close Fairacre at this particular moment?'

'I don't know, but the numbers are dwindling. We're down to twenty-six this term, and somehow there was a look in Mr Salisbury's eye which I didn't like.'

'He's always got that,' said George cheerfully. 'Comes of working in an office all day.' He put down his glass and sprang nimbly to his feet.

I sighed and rose too.

'You sound uncommonly sad,' he said. 'Old age?'

'Probably. How long notice would I get, do you think, if they do decide to close?'

'Years.'

'Honestly? Really *years*?'

'I believe so. Why, you'd probably be about to retire anyway by the time they get round to it.'

We walked together towards the church. The lime trees buzzed with scores of bees, and the scent from the creamy flowers was delicious – the essence of summer. Fairacre seemed very dear and sweet.

'You've got a good spot here,' said George, as if reading my thoughts.

'None better,' I told him, as bravely as I could.

10. WHO SHALL IT BE?

One afternoon, towards the end of term, four candidates for the post of infants' teacher arrived for interview.

It was a sweltering day. The distant downs shimmered in a haze of heat, and the flowers drooped in the border. Tibby had found a cool spot among some thick grass under the hedge, and lay comatose. Even the sparrows were too exhausted to twitter from the school gutters.

Mrs Rose was taking charge of the school for an hour while I attended the interviewing session in my own dining-room, grudgingly polished by Mrs Pringle.

I had hoped that Mrs Rose might feel like applying for the post. She was not ideal, I know, but better the rogue one knew than the devil one didn't. However, since the row with Mrs Pringle, I was relieved to know that she would be leaving at the end of term, as had first been arranged. The frosty silences and cutting looks, which occurred when they met, may have given them some warped satisfaction, but I found the whole business extremely distasteful and childish.

The vicar, as chairman of the managers, was being supported by Peter Hale. As a retired man, he seemed freer than the other managers, and anyway his experience and wisdom, as a school-master, should prove a help on this occasion.

I had had the job of making a short list from the surprisingly large number of applicants for this modest post. It was a sign of the times, of course, as so many teachers were out of work. Normally, we are lucky, at Fairacre, to get two or three applicants. This time there were over fifty, and it had been difficult to choose four for interview.

They were all young. For too long we have had elderly ladies in charge of our youngest children, and though their motherly qualities were endearing, I felt that we were falling behind in up-to-date methods of teaching. It was time to have a change.

From my own point of view too, I wanted someone who could be trained towards my aims with the children. It is doubly important to have a united team when the staff is small, and I was getting heartily sick of trying to keep the boat up straight with people like Mrs Rose who were set in their ways before they even came to Fairacre, and who had no intention of changing them.

Two of the applicants had been teaching for two or three years. The others had just finished their training and would be in their probationary year if they were appointed. We saw these first.

'Charming girls,' said the vicar enthusiastically, as the second one closed the door behind her.

'They are indeed,' agreed Peter Hale. Both girls were remarkably pretty, and I began to wonder if I were going to get an unbiased assessment of their teaching powers from two males who, although elderly, were clearly still susceptible to female good looks.

The first, a fresh-faced blonde, had answered our questions with intelligence, but was not very forthcoming about methods she would use in teaching reading and number, which I found slightly daunting. She was engaged to be married, but intended to go on teaching for a few years before thinking of starting a family.

The second, Hilary Norman, was a red-head, with the creamy pallor of complexion which so often accompanies auburn hair. Her paper qualifications were very good, and she was thoughtful in her answering. Her judgement, in my opinion, was in advance of her years, and she seemed to have a delightful sense of humour. I warmed to her at once, and said so to my fellow-interviewers.

'She'll have to get digs near by,' observed Peter Hale, studying her address. 'Home is somewhere in Herefordshire. Too far to travel. Know anyone in Caxley who might put her up?'

'Not a soul,' I said.

'And really there's no one now in the village,' lamented the vicar. 'And the bus service gets worse and worse.'

'I think we ought to see the others before going any further,' said Peter Hale. 'Let's have Mrs Cornwall, shall we?'

We turned our papers over, and the vicar ushered in the lady.

To my eyes, she seemed just as attractive as the other two, and I could see that I should easily be out-classed in looks next term – not that that would take much doing, I am the first to admit.

She was very calm and composed, and I could well imagine that the infants would behave angelically in her care. But, as the questioning went on, I began to wonder if she would be able to

stimulate them enough. Country children are often inarticulate
– not dumb by any means, they often chatter quite as volubly as
their town cousins – but they are not as facile in expressing
themselves and are basically more reserved.

She had wonderful references, drove her own car, and I felt
she would be a loyal aide. But would she stay in Fairacre long
enough to be of use?

'If my husband is posted abroad, of course I shall go too, but
it might not be for another two years.'

It clinched matters for me, I fear.

The last applicant was amazonian in build, and if anything
even better-looking than those who had gone before. She would
be jolly useful, I thought, in forcing open the high windows
which so often stuck fast at Fairacre School, and her appearance alone would cause respect among her pupils. One
sharp slap from that outsize hand would be enough to settle the
most belligerent infant.

Again, her qualifications were outstanding, and she excelled
in all kinds of sport. This worked both ways, of course, in our
tiny school. Would she miss team games? Would there be
enough scope for her with small children, and a small class of
them at that? I had the feeling that she would be happier in the
livelier atmosphere of a large school, and would find Fairacre
too confining before long.

It was certainly a problem that faced us, when at last she had
returned to await her fate in my sitting-room.

'Fine-looking set of girls,' said Peter Hale. 'Must be something to do with all that National Dried Milk they were
brought up on.'

'I thought that finished years ago,' I said.

'I've never even heard of it,' admitted the vicar. 'Is it the same
as pasteurized?'

This is the way decisions get made in village life, and only a
fool would get impatient with the meandering paths that lead
to our end, but Peter Hale brought us back to the point.

'Perhaps it would be sensible to use the eliminating method

here. We've four excellent candidates. Has Miss Read any doubts about any of them?'

'After all,' put in the vicar, 'you have to work with the lady, and at close quarters. You must find her compatible.'

'Well, I feel that the married lady won't stay long. She was quite frank about it, and it seems as though she fully expects her husband to be sent overseas within two or three years. I'd sooner have someone willing to stay longer.'

'Agreed,' said my two colleagues, putting aside one set of papers.

'And in a way, that goes for the engaged girl too, although I'm sure she would be able to give a reasonable length of service.'

'I liked that little red-haired girl,' confessed the vicar. 'She is so lively. I'm sure the children would respond to her.'

'But we haven't gone steadily through our eliminating yet,' protested Peter Hale. 'Let's be methodical.'

'My dear fellow, I do apologize,' said the vicar, flustered. 'How far had we got? Not the married one, wasn't it?'

'Provisionally,' I agreed guardedly.

'Nor the engaged one? Really, it looks as though you disapproved of matrimony, Miss Read! A holy state, we're told, a holy state!'

'My mind is open, I hope. I just think she is less quick than Miss Norman. She was pretty vague about methods she would use, and I suspect the children might find her too easygoing and get out of hand.'

'Right!' said Peter Hale, putting aside another set of papers.

The vicar sighed.

'She had a remarkably sweet expression, I thought. Reminded me of the early Italian Madonnas.'

'What about the large lady?' asked Peter, ignoring the vicar's gentle lamentations.

'Useful type,' I said. 'Could do all the jobs Mr Willet can't manage. Why, she could lift Mrs Pringle up with one hand!'

'If that should ever be called for,' agreed Peter gravely. 'But what about working with her? Her qualifications are excellent, and she looks in spanking health.'

'I have a feeling that she would find Fairacre a little constricting. She's obviously cut out for a much more demanding post, a bigger staff, older children and so on. There's not enough scope for her here. I wouldn't mind betting that she'll be a head teacher in a big school within ten years. It's like putting a lion in a rabbit hutch.'

'But why did she apply then?' asked the vicar.

'Not enough jobs going.'

'I'm sure that's it,' I said. 'And we shall find that it's a sidestep for this girl, that she'll regret it herself before long.'

'Then that leaves Miss Norman whom you liked from the first. Still feel the same?'

I closed my eyes and thought again. It really is a staggering decision to make, this choosing someone to share one's life so closely in a remote school. Things can so easily go wrong.

I remembered Miss Jackson who had been with me some years earlier. It had been a disastrous appointment, and yet just as much care had gone into considering her.

The fact is that it is virtually impossible to sum up a person until you have lived and worked with them through good times and bad. Paper qualifications, references, examination successes, can only play a small part, and one interview, with the applicant highly nervous and on her best behaviour, can tell little more. Much must be taken on trust.

'Well?' said the vicar and Peter together.

I opened my eyes.

'Yes,' I said. 'I'd like Hilary Norman, if you feel the same.'

'I think it's the best choice,' said Peter.

'Without doubt,' said the vicar. 'And so pretty.'

He turned to Peter. 'Would you like to ask her in again, and apprise the unsuccessful candidates of the result?'

Peter took it like a man. 'I'll go and break it gently,' he said, and vanished to carry the good – and bad – news to the waiting four.

*

Amy came over that evening, bearing a beautiful bouquet of roses from her garden, and the news that Vanessa had produced a son and heir, weighing eleven pounds.

'Good grief!' I exclaimed. 'Poor girl! How is she?'

'Absolutely fine amidst all the rejoicing. It all sounds delightfully feudal, I must say. Tarquin rang last night amidst sounds of revelry in the background, and a bonfire to beat all bonfires blazing on the hill, or ben. Is it "*ben*"?'

'Either that or "butt",' I told her. 'I'm not conversant with the lingo. But tell me more.'

'She had what is euphemistically termed "a good time", I gather.'

'Meaning what?'

'Oh, sheer unadulterated misery for twenty-four hours instead of forty-eight or more. But she's remarkably resilient, you know. Takes after Eileen who thought nothing of a twelve-mile walk as a girl. Uphill at that.'

'And what is he going to be called?'

'Donald Andrew Fraser Tarquin. One thing, people will know the land of his birth.'

'But the initials spell DAFT,' I pointed out. 'He'll have hell at school.'

Amy looked shocked. 'How right you are! What a blessing you noticed it! I shall let Vanessa know at once.'

She put her head on one side, and considered me carefully. I waited for her usual derogatory comments on some facet of my appearance.

'You know, you are remarkably astute in some ways.'

I began to preen myself. I so seldom receive a compliment from Amy.

'It's a pity you're so pig-headed with it,' she added.

I rose with dignity. 'Come and help me put these roses in water,' I said. 'I intend to ignore that quite unnecessary last remark.'

'Hoity-toity,' said Amy, following me into the kitchen, and watching me start my flower arranging.

'Are you going to see Vanessa?'

'Yes, quite soon. James has to go to Glasgow on business, and we thought we'd have the weekend with them. There's one thing about being a Scottish laird. It seems that there are hosts of old loyal retainers to help with the cooking and housework. Why, Vanessa even has an under-nurse to help the monthly one! Can you imagine such luxury?'

'Would you take the matinée jacket I've just finished? It's pink, of course, but that's like life.'

'No bother at all,' said Amy. 'By the way, do you really want that red rose just there?'

'Why not?'

'It breaks the line.'

'What line?'

'Aren't you taking the eye down from that dark bud at the top to the base of the receptacle and below?'

'Not as far as I know. I was simply making sure that they were all in the water.'

Amy sighed. 'I do wish I could persuade you to come to the floral classes with me. It seems so dreadful to see you so ignorant of the basic skills of arrangement. You could really benefit with some pedestal work. Those roses call out for a pedestal.'

'At the price pedestals are, according to Mrs Mawne, these roses can go on calling out,' I said flatly. 'What's wrong with this nice white vase?'

'You're quite incorrigible,' said Amy, averting her eyes. 'By the way, how's Minnie Pringle?'

'In smashing form, as the music hall joke has it.'

I told her about some of Minnie's choicer efforts, particularly the extraordinary methods used for the drying of dusters.

'You won't believe this,' I told her, 'but last Friday she had upturned the vegetable colander on the draining board, and had draped a wet duster over that. Honestly, I give up!'

'Perhaps you won't have her much longer. I hear that Mrs Fowler has ejected Minnie's husband. My window cleaner says the rows could be heard at the other side of Caxley.'

My spirits rose, then fell again. 'But it doesn't mean that he'll come back to Springbourne necessarily, and in any case, Minnie will probably still need a job. I don't dare hope that she'll leave me.'

'He'll have to sleep somewhere,' Amy pointed out, 'and obviously his old home is the place.'

'Minnie might demand more money, though, and let him stay on sufferance,' I said, clinging to this straw like a drowning beetle, 'then she wouldn't need to come to me on Fridays.'

'I think you are going too fast,' said Amy, lighting a cigarette and inserting it into a splendid amber holder. 'It's a case of wishful thinking, as far as you are concerned. I imagine that he'll return to Minnie, make sure she's bringing in as much money as possible, and will sit back and pretend he's looking for work. Minnie really isn't strong enough to protest, is she?'

Sadly, I agreed. It looked as though I could look forward to hundreds of home-wrecking Friday afternoons.

'Mrs Coggs,' I said wistfully, 'is doing more cleaning now that Arthur's inside. I gather she's a treasure.'

'You shouldn't have been so precipitate in offering Minnie a job,' reproved Amy. 'Incidentally, Arthur's case comes up at Crown Court this week. It was in the local paper.'

'I missed that. Actually this week's issue was handed by that idiotic Minnie to Mrs Pringle to wrap up the chickens' scraps, before I'd read it.'

'Typical!' commented Amy, blowing a perfect smoke ring, an accomplishment she acquired at college along with many other distinctions, academic and otherwise.

'Well, if you've quite finished ramming those roses into that quite unsuitable vase,' said Amy, 'can I beg a glass of water?'

'I'll do better than that,' I told her, bearing my beautiful bouquet into the sitting-room. 'There's a bottle of sherry some-where – if Minnie hasn't used it for cleaning the windows.'

11. Problems

As always, everything seemed to happen within the last two weeks of term.

At the beginning of every school year, I make all sorts of good resolutions about being methodical, in time with returning forms and making out lists, arranging programmes well in advance and so on. I have a wonderful vision of myself, calm and collected, sailing through the school year's work with a serene smile, and accepting graciously the compliments of the school managers and the officials at the local education department, on my efficiency.

This blissful vision remains a mirage. I flounder my way through the multitudinous jobs that surround me, and can always still be far behind, particularly with the objectionable clerical work, when the end of the year looms up.

So it was this July. The village fête, in aid of Church Funds as usual, had to have a contribution from the school, and as Mrs Rose became less and less capable as the end of her time drew nigh, and more and more morose since the tiff with Mrs Pringle, I was obliged to work out something single-handed.

It is difficult to plan a programme which involves children from five to eleven taking part, but with all the parents present at the fête, and keen to see their own offspring in the limelight, it was necessary to evolve something.

After contemplating dancing, a play, a gymnastic display and various other hoary old chestnuts, I decided that each of these activities needed more time and rehearsing than I could possibly manage. In the end I weakly fell back on folk songs, most of which the children knew already.

Mrs Rose gave half-hearted support to this proposal, and the air echoed each afternoon as we practised. Meanwhile, there were the usual end of term chores to do, and the heat continued, welcome to me, but inducing increasing languor in the children.

It was during this period that Arthur Coggs and his partners in crime appeared at Crown Court.

As Mr Willet had forecast, all the accused were given prison sentences. The brothers Bryant were sent down for three years and Arthur Coggs for two.

'Not that he'll be there all that time,' said Mr Willet. 'More's the pity. They takes off the time he's been in custody already, see, and if he behaves himself he'll get another few months cut off his spell inside. I reckons he's been lucky this time. We'll have him back in Fairacre before we've got time to turn round, darn it all!'

Mrs Coggs, it was reported, had gone all to pieces on hearing the sentence.

Mrs Pringle told me the details with much relish. 'As a good neighbour,' she said, 'I lent that poor soul the *Caxley Chronicle* to read the result for herself, and I've never seen a body look so white and whey-faced as what she did! Nearly fell off of her chair with the shock,' said Mrs Pringle with evident satisfaction.

'Wouldn't it have been kinder to have told her yourself, if she'd asked?'

'I didn't trust myself not to break down,' responded the old humbug smugly. 'A woman's heart's a funny thing, you know, and she loves that man of hers despite his little failings.'

'I should think "little failings" hardly covers Arthur's criminal activities,' I said, but Mrs Pringle was in one of her maudlin moods and oblivious to my astringency.

'I was glad to see the tears come,' went on that lady. 'I says to her: "That's right! A good cry will ease that breaking heart"!'

'Mrs Pringle,' I cried, 'for pity's sake spare me all this senti-mental mush! Mrs Coggs knew quite well that Arthur would go to prison, and she knew he deserved it. If I'd been in her shoes, I'd have breathed a sigh of relief.'

Mrs Pringle, cut short in the midst of her dramatic tale, looked at me with loathing.

'There's some,' she said, 'as has no feeling heart for the mis-fortunes of others. It's plain to see it would be useless to come to you in trouble, and I'm glad poor Mrs Coggs had my shoulder to weep on in her time of affliction. One of these fine days, you may be in the same boat,' she added darkly, and limped from the room.

Heaven help me, I thought, if that day should ever come.

As it happened, trouble did come, but I managed to cope with-out weeping on Mrs Pringle's ample bosom.

I received a letter from the Office, couched in guarded terms, about the authority's long-term policy of closing small schools which were no longer economic to run. It pointed out that Fairacre's numbers had dwindled steadily over the years, that the matter had been touched on at the last managers' meeting, and that local comment would be sought. It emphasized the fact that nothing would be done without thorough consultation with all concerned, and that this was simply a preparatory exploration of local feeling. Closure, of course, might never take place should numbers increase, or other circumstances make the school vital to the surroundings. But should it be deemed necessary to close, then the children would probably attend Beech Green School, their nearest neighbour.

A copy of the letter, it added, had been sent to all the managers.

I felt as though I had been pole-axed, and poured out my second cup of coffee in a daze.

The rooks were wheeling over the high trees, calling harshly as they banked and turned against the powder-blue morning sky. The sun glinted on their polished feathers as they enjoyed the Fairacre air. How long should I continue to enjoy it, I wondered?

By the time I had sipped the coffee to the dregs, I was feeling calmer. In a way, it is always better to know the worst, than to await tidings in a state of dithering suspense. Well, now something had happened. The rumours were made tangible. The ostrich on the merry-go-round had come to a stop in full view of all of us. Now we must do something about it.

I washed up the breakfast things, put down Tibby's mid-morning snack, washed my hands, and made my way across to the school.

Now what should I choose for our morning hymn? 'Oft in danger, oft in woe' might fit the case, or 'Fight the good fight' perhaps?

No, let's have something bold and brave that we could roar out together!

I opened the book at:

'Ye holy angels bright

Who wait at God's right hand'

and looked with approval at the lines.

'Take what He gives, and praise Him still.

Through good or ill, whoever lives.'

That was the spirit, I told myself, as the children burst in, breathless and vociferous, to start another day beneath the ancient roof which had looked down upon their parents and their grandparents at their schooling years before.

I guessed that the vicar would pay me a visit, and before playtime he entered, holding his letter, and looking forlorn. The children clattered to their feet, glad, as always, of a diversion.

'Sit down, dear children,' said the vicar, 'I mustn't disturb your work.'

That, I thought, is just what they want disturbed, and watched them settle down again reluctantly to their ploys.

'I take it you have had this letter, too?'

'Yes, indeed.'

'It really is most upsetting. I know it stresses the point of there being no hurry in any of these decisions. Nevertheless, I feel we must call an extra-ordinary meeting of the managers, to which you, naturally, are invited, and after that I suppose we may need to have a public meeting in the village. What do you think?'

'See what the managers decide, but I'm sure that's what they will think the right and proper thing to do. After all, it's not only the parents, though they are the most acutely involved, but everyone in Fairacre.'

'My feelings exactly.'

He sighed heavily, and the letter which he had put on my desk, sailed to the floor. Six children fell upon it, like starving dogs upon a crust, and it was a wonder it was not torn to shreds before the vicar regained his property.

After this invigorating skirmish, they returned to their desks much refreshed. The clock said almost a quarter to eleven, and I decided that early playtime was permissible under the circumstances.

They clattered into the lobby and the clanging of milk bottles, taken from the metal crate there, made a background to our conversation.

'You see there was some foundation for those rumours,' commented Mr Partridge. 'No smoke without fire, as they say.'

'It began to look ominous when the measuring started at Beech Green,' I responded. 'And Mr Salisbury was decidedly cagey, I thought. Oh dear, I hope to goodness nothing happens! In a way, the very fact that it's going to be a long drawn-out affair makes it worse. I keep wondering if I should apply for a post elsewhere, before I'm too old to be considered.'

The vicar looked shocked. 'My dear girl, you mustn't think of it! The very idea! *Of course* you must stay here, and we shall all see that you do. That's why I propose to go back to the vicarage and fix a date for the managers' meeting as soon as possible.'

'I do appreciate your support,' I said sincerely, 'it's just this ghastly hanging about. You know.

"The mills of God grind slowly
But they grind exceeding small."'

The vicar's kind old face took on a look of reproof. 'It isn't God's mill that's doing the grinding,' he pointed out. 'It's the Education Office's machinery. And that,' he added vigorously, 'we must put a spoke in.'

If he had been a Luddite he could not have sounded more militant. I watched him cross the playground, with affection and hope renewed.

They say that troubles never come singly, and while I was still reeling under the blow of that confounded letter, I had an unnerving encounter with Minnie Pringle.

Usually, she would have departed when I returned to my home after school on Fridays. I would then remove the wet dusters from whatever crack-brained place Minnie had left them in, put any broken shards in the dustbin, and set about brewing a much-needed cup of tea, thanking my stars that my so-called help had gone home.

But on this particular Friday she was still there when I entered the house. A high-pitched wailing greeted me, and going to investigate I found Minnie sitting on the bottom stair with a broken disinfectant bottle at her feet.

She was rocking herself back and forth, occasionally throwing her skirt over her mop-head of red hair, and displaying deplorable underwear including a pair of tights more ladders than fabric.

I was reminded suddenly of those Irish plays where the stage is almost too murky to see what is happening, the only light being focused dimly on a coffin with four candles, one at each corner, and a gaggle of keening women, while a harp is being plucked, in lugubrious harmony, by some unseen hand.

'What on earth's the matter, Minnie? Don't cry about a broken bottle. We can clear that up.'

'It ain't the *bottle*!' wailed Minnie, pitching herself forward with renewed energy.

'What is it then?'

She flung herself backward, hitting her head on the fourth stair up. I hoped it might knock some sense into her.

'Ah-ah-ah-ah!' yelled Minnie, and flung her skirt over her head once more.

I took hold of her skinny shoulders and shook her. The screaming stopped abruptly, and the skirt was thrown back over the dreadful tights.

'Now stop all this hanky-panky,' I said severely, 'and tell me what's wrong.'

Snivelling, Minnie took up the hem of her skirt once more, but this time applied it to her weeping eyes and wet nose. I averted my gaze hastily.

'Come on, Minnie,' I said, more gently. 'Come and have a cup of tea with me. You'll feel better.'

She sniffed, and shook her head. 'Gotter clear up this bottle as broke,' she said dimly.

'Well, let's find the dustpan and you do that while I make the tea.'

She accompanied me to the kitchen, still weeping, but in a less hysterical fashion. I found the dustpan – for some reason, best known to Minnie, among the saucepans – and handed it over with a generous length of paper towel to mop up her streaming face. I then propelled her into the hall, and returned to prepare the tea tray.

'At this rate,' I muttered to myself, 'I shall need brandy rather than tea.'

Five minutes later, sitting at the kitchen table, the tale unfolded in spasmodic fashion.

'It's Ern,' said Minnie. 'He's comin' back.'

Ern, I knew, was the husband who had so recently deserted her.

'And you don't want him?'

'Would you?'

'No!' I said, without hesitation. 'But can't you tell him so?'

'What, Ern? He'll hit me if I says that.'

'Well, get the police.'

'He'll hit me worse if I tells them.'

I changed my tactics. 'Are you sure he's going to come back?'

'He wrote to Auntie – she can read, you see – and said his place was at my side.'

'What a nerve!' I exclaimed. 'It hasn't been for the last few months, has it?'

'Well, it's different now. That Mrs Fowler don't want 'im. She's turned 'im out.'

So Amy was right after all, I thought.

'And when's he supposed to be coming?'

Minnie let out another ear-splitting yell, and I feared that we were in for another period of hysteria.

'Tonight, 'e says. And I'm too afeared to go home. And what will Bert say?'

'Bert?' I echoed, in perplexity.

'My boy friend what works up Springbourne Manor.' Minnie looked coy.

I remembered the rumour about the under-gardener who had been consoling Minnie in her loneliness.

'What about Bert?'

'He'll hit him too,' said Minnie.

'Your husband will?'

'Yes. Bound to. And Bert'll 'it 'im back, and there'll be a proper set-to.'

Minnie's fears seemed to be mingled with a certain pleasurable anticipation at the prospect, it seemed to me.

'Well you'd better let Bert know what's happening,' I said, 'and he can keep away. That is, if Ern comes at all. Perhaps he's only making threats.'

Minnie's eyes began to fill again. 'He'll come all right. He ain't got nowhere to sleep, see. And I dursn't face him. He'll knock me about terrible, and the kids. What am I to do?'

'You say Mrs Pringle had the letter?'

'Yes. She read it out to me.'

'She'll be over at the school now,' I said, putting down my cup. 'I'll go and see her while you have some more tea.'

I left her, still sniffing, and sought out her aunt, who was balanced on a desk top dusting the partition between the two classrooms.

'My, what a start you gave me!' she gasped, one hand on her heart.

'Can you come down for a minute?' I said, holding out my hand for support. 'It's about Minnie.'

Mrs Pringle, twisting my hand painfully, descended in a crab-wise fashion, and sat herself on the front desk. I faced her, propped on my table.

'She's in tears about that husband of hers, and seems afraid to go home.'

'I knows that. She's been no better than she should be while he's been away. He's promised her a thundering good 'iding.'

'But he's threatening her just because he wants somewhere to sleep. It all seems most unfair to me. After all, he left her.'

'Maybe. But his place is in his own home, with Minnie.'

'But, he's intimidating her!'

'Natural, ain't it? How else did she get her last baby?'

I felt unequal to explaining the intricacies of the English language to Mrs Pringle, and let it pass.

'The point is, Mrs Pringle, that it really wouldn't be safe to let her go home if he intends to come and knock her about. Should we tell the police?'

Mrs Pringle bridled. 'What, and let the neighbours have a free show? Not likely.'

'But the children—'

Mrs Pringle's face became crimson with wrath. She thrust her head forward until our noses were almost touching.

'Are you trying to tell me what to do with Minnie's children? I'll tell you straight, I'm not having that tribe settling on me with all I've got to do. I'm sick and tired of Minnie and her lot, and the sooner she pushes off and faces up to the trouble she's made the better.'

'So you won't help?'

'I've done nothing but help that silly girl, and I'm wore out with it.'

'I can understand that, and I think you've been remarkably patient. But now what's to be done? I really think the police should be warned that there might be trouble.'

Mrs Pringle's breathing became heavy and menacing.

'You just try it! You dare! I've been thinking about the best way to tackle this ever since I got that Ern's letter. He can talk – going off with that old trollop who's old enough to be his mother!'

I began to feel dizzy. Whose side was Mrs Pringle on?

'What I'm going to do,' said my cleaner, 'is to go back with Minnie and the kids tonight, and to sleep the night at her place, with the rolling pin on one side of me and the poker on the other. I'll soon settle that Ern's hash if he dares put a foot inside the place. We don't need no police, Miss Read, that I can tell you!'

'Splendid!' I cried. 'Can I go and tell Minnie?'

'Yes. And I'll be ready to set off in half an hour sharp, tell her, just as soon as I've got the cobwebs off this partition.'

She heaved herself up on to the desk again, duster in hand, and I returned home, thinking what a wonderfully militant band we were in Fairacre, from the vicar to Mrs Pringle.

12. MILITANT MANAGERS

The extra-ordinary managers' meeting was called during the last week of term, and great difficulty the vicar had encountered before gathering them all together.

The long hot spell had advanced harvest, and Mr Roberts was already in that annual fever which afflicts farmers at this time of year when the vicar rang. However, he nobly put aside his panic and agreed to spend an hour away from his combine harvester, as the matter seemed urgent.

Mrs Lamb was supposed to be at a flower arranging meeting at Caxley where someone, of whom Mrs Lamb spoke with awe in her voice, was going to show her respectful audience how to make Large Displays for Public Places from no more than five bought flowers and the bounty culled from the hedgerows. Mrs Lamb, whose purse was limited but who enjoyed constructing enormous decorations of bulrushes, reeds, branches, honesty and even beetroot and rhubarb leaves, was looking forward to learning more, but gave up the pleasure to do her duty.

Mrs Mawne had a bridge party arranged at her house, but was obliged to do a great deal of telephoning to get it transferred to another player's. As all the ladies vied with each other in preparing exotic snippets of food to have with their tea, this meant even further domestic complications. However, it was done.

Mrs Moffat was busy putting the final touches to a magnificent ball dress which was destined to go to a Masonic Ladies' Night, but set aside her needle to be present, while Peter Hale, recently retired from the local grammar – now comprehensive –

school, cursed roundly at ever being fool enough to agree to being a manager when the grass wanted cutting so urgently.

Resigned to their lot, therefore, they assembled in the vicar's dining-room one blazing afternoon and accepted a cup of tea from Mrs Partridge before she departed to her deckchair under the cedar tree, there to read, or rather to skip through, the final chapters of a very nasty book, strongly recommended by the book critics of the Sunday papers, and dealing with the incestuous relations of a sadistic father and his equally repulsive teenage daughter. The fact, much advertised by the publishers, that it had already sold thirty thousand copies and was now reprinting, gave Mrs Partridge more cause for regret than rejoicing, but she was determined to turn over the pages until the end, so that she could give her trenchant comments on the work, and truthfully say she 'had been through it', in more ways than one.

No one appeared from the Office on this occasion, but I was invited, and enjoyed my cup of tea, and the comments of the managers.

'We've got to be firm about this,' said Mr Roberts. 'Say "No" from the outset. I mean, what's village life coming to?'

'How do you mean?' asked Mrs Moffat.

'Well, we used to have a village bobby. Remember Trumper, padre?'

The vicar said he did, and what a splendid fellow he was.

'Exactly. Used to hear old Trumper puffing round the village every night about two o'clock making sure everything was in order.'

'So sensible,' agreed Mrs Mawne. 'We need more police. That's half the trouble these days.'

'And what's more,' went on Mr Roberts, 'he gave any young scallywag a good clip round the ear-'ole, on the spot, and stopped a peck of wrong-doing. What happens now? Some ruddy Juvenile Court six months later when the kid's forgotten all about it.'

The vicar coughed politely. 'Quite. We take your point, but it is the school closure we are considering.'

'It's the same principle,' said Peter Hale, coming to Mr Roberts' support 'You need direct contact – that's the unique quality of village life. If we lose the village bobby it's a link broken. Far worse to lose our village school.'

'Too little spread too thin,' said Mrs Lamb. 'Same as having to share you, Mr Partridge, with Beech Green and Springbourne. Why, I remember the time, before your day, of course, when the vicar was just for Fairacre, and you could reckon to see him any time you wanted, if you were in trouble. He'd be in his study or the garden, or in the church or visiting in the parish. Now he can be anywhere.'

The vicar nodded and looked unhappy.

'Not that it can be altered,' added Mrs Lamb hastily, 'and a marvellous job you do, but nevertheless, it's not the same.'

'I suppose there's no hope of this school staying open for infants only?' asked Mrs Mawne. 'The biggest objection is hauling the babies to Beech Green, I think.'

'It's too small as it is,' I said. 'Even if the Beech Green infants were brought here, both schools would still be too small according to the authority.'

The arguments went on. I was touched to see how concerned they all were, not only for the children's sake and mine, but for the destruction of a tradition which went back for over a hundred years.

'If we give in,' said Mr Roberts, 'we're betraying the village, as I see it. Our Fairacre children get a jolly sound grounding. You've only got to look at the percentage we used to get through the eleven-plus exam to go on to the grammar school, before it turned into this blighted whatever it's called. I propose we send a reply to the Office saying we're firmly against the idea of closure.'

This proposal was carried unanimously, and the vicar promised to write the letter that evening.

The clock stood at four-thirty. Mr Roberts rushed back to his combine, Mrs Moffat to her ball gown, Mrs Lamb to the telephone to hear all about the flower-arranging from a friend, Mrs Mawne to studying the bridge column in last Sunday's paper in lieu of her game, and Peter Hale to his lawn mower.

I stood in the vicarage garden and looked across at our modest weatherbeaten school across the way.

'Never fear,' said the vicar, clapping me on the shoulder. 'It will be there for another hundred years, believe me.'

'I hope so,' I said soberly.

Amy called in unexpectedly that evening while my head was still humming with the memory of the managers' meeting.

I told her a little about it. To my surprise, she seemed to think that Fairacre School was doomed to close, and that it would be a good thing.

'Well, I'm blowed!' I exclaimed. 'A fine friend you are! I suppose you want to see me queuing up for my dole before long?'

'Well, no,' replied Amy, with what I thought quite unnecessary hesitation. 'Not exactly, but I do think this place is an anachronism.'

'How can it be if it serves a useful purpose in the village?'

'I sometimes wonder if it does. Oh, I know all about fathers and grandfathers doing their pot-hooks and hangers under these very windows, but it's time things changed.'

'My children don't do pot-hooks and hangers.'

'Don't snap, dear. What I'm trying to point out is that things have altered considerably. For one thing, those grandfathers came to Fairacre School when it boasted a hundred children or more, as the log books show. It was a real *school-sized* school then, and enough boys present to play a decent game of football or cricket among themselves if they wanted to.'

'Team games aren't everything.'

'And then this building,' continued Amy, waving a hand. 'It's really had its time, you know. The very fabric is crumbling, as Mrs Pringle points out daily. And those antiquated stoves!

And that ghastly skylight forever letting in rain and a wicked draught! It's really not good enough. I wonder the parents haven't complained before now.'

I was speechless before this onslaught. Perhaps Amy was right. She often was, as I knew to my cost.

I changed the subject.

'You were right about Mrs Fowler by the way. She's pushed out Minnie's husband, and Minnie's afraid he'll come back to her.'

'With that row of children to look after, I should think she might welcome him.'

I told her about Minnie's fears of aggression, and how Mrs Pringle had gone into attack. Amy listened avidly.

'And did he come?'

'No, thank heaven, but they expect him daily and barricade the door with the kitchen table whenever they return home. The children think it is terrific fun.'

'Children are odd,' agreed Amy. 'I remember how Kenneth used to insist on having the more lugubrious parts of *Black Beauty* read to him, while the tears rolled down his cheeks. He was about six then.'

Kenneth was a brother of Amy's who was killed in the last war. I had met him occasionally, and could never take to him, finding him boastful, selfish, and frequently untruthful. He was a confounded nuisance to his parents in his teens, as so many boys are, and they were wonderfully realistic and cheerful about it.

However, no sooner had he died than their attitude to the young man was completely transformed. To hear them talk of Kenneth, after his death, one would have imagined him to be a paragon of all the virtues, kind, noble, a loving son and devoted friend to many. So does death transfigure us. Perhaps it is as well, but personally I think one should cling to the truth – in charitable silence, of course – and not try to deceive oneself, or others, about the rights of the matter.

Even now, so long after, Amy's voice took on a reverent note when Kenneth's name was mentioned. I was glad that she remembered him with love, but wondered if such an out-standingly honest and downright person as dear Amy really conned herself into believing Kenneth the complete hero.

'He was the handsomest of us all,' went on Amy, gazing across the fields outside the window. 'Our Aunt Rose always gave him a better birthday present than the rest of us. We used to resent it dreadfully.'

'Quite natural, I should think.'

'And it's about Aunt Rose I've come tonight,' said Amy, becoming her usual brisk self. 'She died a fortnight ago and I'm clearing out the house for her. When you break up, could you spare a couple of afternoons to help?'

I said I would be glad to.

'It's no joke, I can tell you,' warned Amy. 'She seems to have kept every letter and photograph and Christmas card since about 1910.'

'They'd probably make a fortune at Sotheby's,' I said.

'Make a hefty bonfire,' commented Amy, picking up her handbag. 'Anyway, many thanks for offering. I'll pick you up one afternoon next week, and we'll get down to it. I should bring a large overall and tie up your hair.'

'How's Vanessa?' I said, as Amy slammed the car door.

'Besotted with motherhood,' said Amy. 'I think she's going to be one of those mamas who keep a diary of daily progress. You know the sort of thing:

Thursday: Baby dribbled.
Friday: Baby squinted.
Saturday: Baby burped.'

'It's because it's the first,' I said indulgently.

'Well, her only hope is to have about half a dozen. Surely she would be more reasonable then.'

She drove off, and I returned to prepare a snack for the ever-voracious Tibby.

The last day of term passed off jubilantly, its glory only partly clouded by my secret fears that this might be perhaps the last day of a school year spent under Fairacre School's dilapidated roof.

However, I put such dismal thoughts aside, and fell to tidying cupboards, dismantling the nature table, removing the children's artwork from the walls and ruining my thumb nail as a result, as I do regularly. A broken thumb nail and arthritis in the right shoulder, caused by writing on the blackboard, are just two of a teacher's occupational hazards, I have discovered. Increasing impatience, over the years, seems to be another, certainly in my case.

But today in the golden haze of breaking up, all was well. The children were noisy but busy. The sun blazed down as though it would continue to do so until Christmas. Mr Roberts' combine provided a pleasant humming from some distant field, and a drowsy bumblebee droned up and down one of the school windows.

The afternoon flew by. We stood for grace in the unusually tidy and bare classroom, our voices echoing hollowly, and praised God for mercies received and blessings to come, before the tumultuous rush for home.

Joseph Coggs was the last to leave.

'You want any gardening done this 'oliday?' he asked in his husky voice.

'Why, yes,' I said untruthfully.

It was plain that he needed occupation as well as a little pocket money.

'Can your mother spare you?' I asked. 'Or should you be helping with the baby?'

'The baby goes with 'er,' said Joseph, running a grubby finger along the table edge. 'Anyway the twins does that all right.'

'Well, if you're sure,' I said, making up my mind to have a word with Mrs Coggs before he came, 'then perhaps one morning next week, if it stays fine.'

'Cor!' was all he said, but he raised his dark eyes to mine, and unalloyed delight shone from them.

I patted his shoulder. I have a very soft spot for young Joseph, and life has never treated him well. Despite that, he has a sweetness of disposition which one rarely meets. Things must be pretty grim at home, and pretty tight, too. I should be glad to have him to help, if only to enjoy his obvious pleasure at being of use.

'Off you go then,' I said. 'I'll call at your house soon to fix things up.'

He skipped off, and I followed him.

The sun had beaten down upon the faded paint of the school door all the afternoon, and it was almost too hot to touch. In the distance, the downs trembled through veils of heat haze, and my spirits rose at the thought of weeks of summer holiday stretching before me.

I skipped, almost as blithely as young Joseph, across the playground towards my home.

13. OTHER PEOPLE'S HOMES

As promised, I went to see Mrs Coggs one evening during the first week of the holidays.

I knew better, as a country dweller, than to knock at the front door. In most cases, the knocker is securely fastened by layers of paint and the grime of years, except in the case of those once termed gentry, who still have polished knockers on their front doors, and use them.

The concrete path leading to Mrs Coggs' back door was so narrow and flush with the wall that it was quite a balancing feat to remain on it. The surface was badly cracked, and here and there an iron manhole cover added to the hazards. Fairacre 'went on the mains' a few years ago and we seem to have sprouted more covers than taps in the village.

At the back door three scraggy chickens pecked idly at the concrete, scattering with a squawk when they saw me, and fleeing to cover among some gooseberry bushes almost hidden in long grass. It was apparent that no gardener's hand had been at work here for many a long year, and I wondered if the Council had issued any reprimand about the state of its property.

Mrs Coggs appeared at the door looking like a startled hare. Her eyes bulged and her nose was atwitch.

'I didn't mean to frighten you,' I began.

She wiped her wet hands on the sacking apron which girt her skinny form, and pushed wisps of dank hair from her face.

'You best come in,' she said resignedly, and stepped over the threshold into the kitchen. I followed her.

I nearly stepped straight back again, stunned by the appalling smell. Mrs Coggs was busy wiping the seat of a wooden chair with the useful sacking apron and had her back to me, so that I hoped she had not seen my dismay.

The twins, runny-nosed despite the hot day, now came to the door which led into the other room where most of the living was done. They looked as startled as their mother, and put grimy thumbs into their mouths for comfort.

'Clear off!' said Mrs Coggs. 'Miss Read don't want you lot 'anging around, and no more don't I!'

While I was engaged mentally in correcting the grammar of this last phrase, the two little girls sidled past me nervously, and bolted into the garden. The toddler, who had been hiding behind the back of the sacking apron, now set up a terrible hullabaloo. Mrs Coggs sat down at the kitchen table and hoisted him on to it among towers of dirty saucepans, plates, old newspapers, and a broken colander which seemed to contain a multitude of fish heads. It was this last, I guessed, which contributed the largest and most potent part of the general stench.

'It's gone your bed-time, ain't it, lovey,' she crooned, her face as suffused with tenderness, as she surveyed her youngest, as it had been with exasperation at the sight of the twins only a minute before. I was reminded of mother cats who adore their tiny babies, and cuff them unmercifully as soon as they think they should be off their hands.

'It was about Joe that I've come,' I said. 'I wondered if he could help me in the garden now and again during the holidays.'

She continued to stroke the baby's hair and did not answer. I began to wonder if she were becoming deaf, or if she were still too bemused by her change of fortune to take in anything she was asked. She certainly looked white and pinched, and I wondered if she were getting enough to eat.

'Perhaps one morning a week?' I said. 'He could stop and have his midday dinner with me, if that fits in with your plans.'

The mention of food seemed to rouse her.

'He'd like that. Always likes 'is school dinners, that one. More'n the twins does. They eats next to nothing.'

'What do they like?' I inquired.

'Bread and sauce,' she replied. 'They has that most days. Saves cooking.'

I pointed to the nauseating collection of fish heads. 'Are you going to cook those?' I inquired tentatively.

She surveyed them with some surprise, as though she had only just noticed their presence, although heaven above knew, they made themselves felt quite enough.

'Fishmonger give 'em to me yesterday, and said to boil 'em for soup or summat. But we'd never eat that stuff. I likes tomato out of a tin.'

I could not probe too deeply into Mrs Coggs' culinary arrangements though I was dying to know how she fed the family. Surely they didn't live on bread and sauce exclusively? I returned to Joe's arrangements.

'What about Tuesday mornings?' I suggested.

'Yeh, that's fine. I goes out all day Tuesday charing. I takes the baby, and the twins can come too in the holidays, but I usually leaves 'em 'ere, out of the way.'

'That's settled then,' I said, making my way to the door, and anxious to get a breath of fresh air after the foetid atmosphere inside. Spread over the hedge, I saw some shrunken and torn garments, fit only for polishing rags. Their washing had been sketchy, and they were still stained in many places. The overpowering smell of poverty and neglect saddened me.

'Mrs Coggs,' I said, able to bear it no longer, 'are you being looked after by the Social Security people? I mean, you are getting money regularly?'

Her face lit up. 'I gets over a pound for each kid now and Joe gets a pound too. And there's me own supplementary. I've never 'ad so much in me life. We gotter telly now.'

'But what about food?'

She looked bewildered. 'They has what they likes best. I told you, bread and sauce, and now I buys a few cakes and sweets. We ain't hard up, Miss, if that's what's worrying you. And I've got me work.'

I turned away, sighing. It was quite apparent that Mrs Coggs' home conditions were the result of lack of management rather than lack of money. I guessed that she was brought up in a home as feckless as her own, and marriage to Arthur could not have helped her, but how sad it all seemed! Sad and wasteful!

'Then I'll look forward to seeing Joe next Tuesday,' I said retracing my steps over the manhole covers. 'About ten, shall we say? And I'll send him home about one, after he's had lunch with me.'

She nodded vaguely, and lifted the child from her hip to the ground, where he sat in the dust. His bottom, I noticed, was completely bare. His hand was already reaching for a dollop of dried chicken's mess.

I escaped into the lane, and picked the first sprig of honeysuckle I could find. It mitigated the reek of fish only a little, but it helped.

Amy came to lunch before we both drove over to her late aunt's house, some miles beyond Springbourne, to sort out the old lady's things.

Still worried about the Coggs family, I poured out an account of my visit. Amy remained unperturbed.

'I can't think why you worry yourself so much about other people's affairs,' she said. 'I imagine Mrs Coggs muddles along quite satisfactorily. After all, she's still alive and kicking, and the children too, despite her appalling housekeeping.'

'But it's all so *unnecessary*,' I began.

'It's purely relative,' said Amy, accepting a second helping of gooseberry pie. 'I mean, look at the way I could worry myself stiff about you – but what good would it do?'

'How d'you mean?' I said, bridling.

'Well, the slapdash way you go about things. This pastry for instance. I imagine it's frozen, or something like that?'

'Of course it is. I make ghastly pastry, and the kitchen floor wants a good scrub after I've done it. Why, does it taste horrible? You've had two helpings, so it can't be too bad.'

'I was always brought up,' said Amy, touching her lips delicately with her napkin, 'in the belief that it was excessively rude to comment on the amount eaten by one's guests.'

'Oh, come off it,' I said. 'What I want to know is why you compare me with Mrs Coggs?'

'Simply this. *You* worry about Mrs Coggs because she is so inefficient. I *could* worry about *you* because you, in your way, are just as feckless. Fancy spending all that money on frozen pastry when it would cost you about half to make your own!'

'Don't nag,' I said. 'All right. I take your point, and I'll try not to get too worked up about the bread and sauce menu at the Coggs'. But I shall see Joe gets a decent meal on the days he comes here.'

We washed up amicably, drank a cup of coffee (instant) apiece and drove over the hill towards Aunt Rose's establishment.

There had been a thunderstorm in the night, and the air was fresh and moist. The road ran between thick woods which gave off a delicious scent of wet leaves and moss. A slight mist hung over the little tributary of the Cax at Springbourne, and a flotilla of ducks splashed happily by the humpback bridge.

A magpie flew chattering across the road, just in front of the car.

'*One for sorrow*,' quoted Amy. 'Did you spit?'

'Spit?'

'How ignorant you are! You should always spit if you see a magpie alone. It takes the venom out of the spell.'

'I had no idea you were superstitious.'

'I'm not. But I do spit at one magpie, and I make a cross in spilt salt, of course, and I wouldn't dream of cutting my nails on a Friday, but I wouldn't consider myself superstitious.'

'What about walking under ladders?'

'Common sense not to. Someone might drop a pot of paint over you.'

I pondered on the fact that no matter how long one knows people there still remain depths unplumbed in their make up.

Aunt Rose's house lay some two miles along a narrow and twisted lane. A charm of goldfinches fluttered from the high hedges, bound, I felt sure, for some thistle seeds which were growing near by. A crow was busy pecking at the corpse of a poor squashed hedgehog, victim, no doubt, of a car during its night-time foraging. It was being watched by a pony whose shaggy head hung over a gate. Animals, it seemed, enjoyed each other's company, and were as curious about each other's activities, as any of us village folk at Fairacre.

The house had a forlorn look as we approached it. The curtains were half-drawn and every window tightly shut. It was deathly quiet and still when we went inside, and smelt of dust and old clothes.

'Leave the front door wide open,' directed Amy, 'and let's open a few windows before we go upstairs.'

It had been built in the thirties, when Aunt Rose's father had died, leaving her comfortably off. It was quite a period piece and a very pleasant one too, with its cream walls and paintwork, its fawn tiled hearth, the standard lamp crowned with its beige bell-shaped shade, and the oatmeal-coloured great Knole settee tied at the corners with silk cord.

On the wide window sills stood the sort of flower vases one rarely sees these days – pottery posy rings, a glass bowl containing a heavy glass holder with bored holes, and several fine lustre jugs. On a little table near by lay a half-finished piece of knitting in pale blue wool. It looked like part of a jumper sleeve, and a spider had spun a long gossamer strand across its surface. It brought home to me, with dreadful poignancy, the swift transition from life to death, when our toys are set aside and we have to leave our playing.

We made our way upstairs where a smell of lavender greeted us. A bowl of dried flowers stood on the table on the landing and scented the whole top floor. Amy wanted to go through her aunt's clothes before tackling anything else, and we set to with a will.

Out of the wardrobe came the sort of clothes which a repertory theatre would welcome. There were coats trimmed with silver fox fur, black evening gowns, ablaze with sequins at the neck, and a musquash coat from which flew several moths as we dumped it on the bed.

On the rack at the bottom of the wardrobe we removed beautiful cream kid shoes with Louis heels, and some later ones with stiletto heels and sharply pointed toes. Everything was in apple pie order.

'Now, what I propose to do,' said Amy, 'is to make three piles. One for myself, one for friends and relatives, and one for local jumble sales. Let's make a start.'

It all seemed very well thought out, until we began. Amy's pile was extremely modest. She put aside two almost new tweed skirts and a pretty little fur stole. It was the division of the rest between relatives and jumble which gave us a headache. Amy proved surprisingly dithery over the allotment.

'I think we ought to let the two nieces have a look at these woollies. After all, they're practically new and came from Harrods. Perhaps they're too good for the jumble pile.'

And so they would be transferred, changing places – but only temporarily – with four pairs of elbow-length gloves with rows of pearl buttons.

My head was beginning to buzz by the time Amy called a halt and we went downstairs for a change of occupation.

Aunt Rose, methodical to the last, had left a list of objects which she wanted close friends to have. Our job was to tie on labels bearing the new owner's name.

It was not quite so exhausting as the upstairs sorting, and we duly affixed labels to pieces of beautiful Wedgwood, Venetian glass, a nest of tables, two bronze clocks and a few choice pieces of furniture.

I found the job rather sad. It seemed such a pity that all these lovely things, which had lived together cheek-by-jowl for so many years, should now be parted. But I comforted myself with the thought that no doubt they were going to homes where they would be cherished as dearly as they had been by Aunt Rose.

The sky was overcast as we locked up and drove away.

'More rain tonight,' forecast Amy, dodging a rabbit that sprinted across the narrow lane. 'Bang goes any idea of mowing the lawn tomorrow. Can you come again tomorrow afternoon to finish off upstairs?'

'I've got Joseph Coggs to lunch,' I said, 'but I could be ready by two.'

'You and your gentlemen friends,' commented Amy. 'I only wish this one were more your age and you took him seriously.'

She drew up at the school house, and shook her head when I asked her in.

'No, I must get back. But a thousand thanks for helping. I'll see you tomorrow.'

She let in the clutch, and then shouted over her shoulder as the car moved forward.

'Give Joe a good lunch!'

14 · The Summer Holiday

The clock of St Patrick's was striking ten when Joseph Coggs arrived. The sun was beginning to break through the clouds which had brought more rain at dawn, and gilded the wet paths and sparked tiny rainbows from the droplets on the hedge. My temporary gardener looked remarkably happy.

'Wodjer want doin', miss?' he inquired after our greetings. He surveyed the garden appreciatively.

'What about weeding the border?'

'I likes weedin'!' said Joe, accepting a bucket and small fork, 'but if I don't know which is which I'll 'ave to 'oller to you.'

I agreed that that would be wise, and watched him tackle the job. He was quick and neat in his movements, and the groundsel and twitch were soon mounting in the bucket. There is one thing about neglecting a border. By the time you get down to it the results are really spectacular.

Joe began to hum happily to himself and I returned to the kitchen.

I had prepared a chicken casserole, and as the oven was in use I decided to make a treacle tart, for where would you find a small boy who doesn't like treacle tart? With Amy's rebuke still ringing in my head, I resolved to make my own pastry.

I must admit, I found the task quite rewarding, despite the shower of crumbs which managed to leap from the bowl on to the floor. I found myself becoming quite dreamy as I rolled the pastry. It was such a soporific exercise that I was quite startled when Joe appeared at the open window before me. His eyes were bright as he watched me at work.

'Us havin' poy then?'

'Treacle tart.'

'Cor!' breathed Joe. He rested his elbows on the outside window sill and settled down to watch. It was not long before his gaze became as bemused as I guessed my own was. Perhaps it was the rhythmic movement of the rolling pin, I thought.

'I loves pastry,' growled Joe. 'Bein' made, I mean, as well as when I eats it.'

I nodded in reply, and lifted the floppy material on to a shallow dish.

'Like sittin' by the fire, or sleepin' with your back against your mum,' went on Joe, suddenly loquacious. 'You want that bit what's cut off?'

'No,' I said, handing over a strip. 'But should you eat it raw?'

'Gives you worms, my mum says,' said Joe contentedly, retreating rapidly with his booty, 'but I still likes it.'

He returned to the border leaving me to ponder on the primitive needs which still make themselves felt, and which had given Joe such unusual powers of expression.

The chicken stew was relished as keenly as the treacle tart, and while we were demolishing my handiwork we chatted of this and that, his next gardening spell with me, why rabbits have so many babies, what happens to your inside if you eat soap, why Mrs Partridge has summer curtains as well as winter ones, and other interesting topics.

'Is our school truly going to shut?' he said suddenly, spoon arrested halfway to his mouth. A thread of treacle drooped dangerously tableward, and I steered his hand over his plate.

'I don't know. I hope not.'

'Mrs Pringle told me mum it was going to.'

I should like to have said: 'Don't believe anything Mrs Pringle tells you,' but civility and the enforced camaraderie of those in authority forbade.

'No one knows yet.'

Joe's dark eyes looked troubled. 'Well, I don't want to go off in a bus to that 'ol Beech Green.'

'Why not?'

Joe twirled his spoon slowly, winding up the treacle.

'I'm afeared of that Mr Annett. 'E walloped my cousin Fred 'orrible.'

'He probably misbehaved,' I said primly. 'Mr Annett doesn't punish children unless they've been really bad.'

'Well, I'm not going anyways,' said Joe, looking mutinous. 'I 'ates going on buses away from Fairacre.'

'Why? Do you feel ill?'

'No. But I bin to Caxley sometimes, and to Barrisford on the outings, and I don't like it. I don't like being so far away.'

I remembered his look when he described the comfort of sleeping with his back against his mother.

'I likes to be home,' he sighed. 'It's right to be home. It's safe there.'

The vision of that appalling kitchen rose before me, the stinking fish heads in the colander, the dirty rags on the draining board, the grease on the floor, the meals of bread and sauce consumed at that filthy table. But to Joe it meant happiness.

Miss Clare, I remembered, had a sampler hanging on her cottage wall, by the fireplace.

'*Home is where the heart is*' it said in cross-stitch. It certainly seemed to apply in the case of Joseph Coggs.

I told Amy about Joe's disclosure as we continued to sort out Aunt Rose's effects that afternoon.

'It seems to me that everyone in Fairacre is taking it for granted that the school is going to close,' I said, holding up a pair of vicious-looking corsets with yards of pink lacings hanging from them.

Amy took them from me and deposited them on the jumble pile.

'Well, what do you expect? After all, it affects everybody and you know what village life is like, better than most. If there isn't a real drama going on then someone will invent one.'

'But nothing has been decided yet.'

'All the more fun. You can make your own ending, can't you? I suppose you realize that you are the central character?'

'How? I've said nothing.'

'A dispossessed person, you'll be. The evicted innocent cast out into the snow, frail, noble and uncomplaining. The village is dying to rally to your support.'

'That'll be the day!'

'Or maybe you'll be rescued, just in time to save you from complete penury, by some gallant hero who marries you in Fairacre church while the children throw rose petals in your path.'

'Lumps of coke, more likely, knowing them.'

I held up a vest which looked remarkably short. 'What's this?'

'A *spencer*, dear. It's time they came back. You wear it under or over your petticoat in cold weather. A very sensible garment. Put it on my pile. It'll be just the thing for next winter.'

I did as I was bid.

'I hope you're wrong,' I went on, 'about village feelings. Lord knows there's enough to keep all the gossip-mongers busy at the moment, what with Minnie Pringle's affairs, and Mrs Pringle's spasmodic dieting, and talk of Dr Martin retiring at last, and Mr Lamb's brother and his family coming over from America very soon, and the mystery of two dead rats in the rainwater butt outside the vestry door.'

Amy broke into a peal of laughter, and sat down on the side of the bed clutching a black velvet evening cape to her ribs.

'Heavens, how you do go on in Fairacre,' she managed to gasp. 'No wonder you don't want to leave with all that happening around you! But, mark my words, there will still be time left to attend to you and your affairs, even if they do have to compete with two dead rats in the vestry's rainwater butt.'

She shook out the velvet cape and studied it with her head on one side. 'For bridge parties, should you think?'

'For the jumble pile,' I told her.

And, for once, she obeyed.

*

A few days later, I set off for a short holiday in East Anglia, staying with friends and revisiting on my way to Norfolk the little resort of Walton-on-the-Naze where I had stayed as a child with my grandparents. The air was still as bracing as I remembered it from my youth, and I felt no desire to plunge into the chilly waves of the North Sea, despite the sunshine.

I forgot my cares as I travelled. It was a relief to leave all the gossipers to get on with their tongue-wagging and wonderful not to have to guard my own conversation. I returned to Fairacre, after nine days of enjoyment, much refreshed.

It was Mrs Pringle's day for 'doing' me, and she was in the kitchen when I went in, doing something complicated with an old toothbrush at the sink.

'A dirt-trap, these 'ere taps,' was her greeting. 'I'd like to meet the fellow as designed 'em. No room to get behind 'em to scrub out the filth. And filth you can always reckon to find in this kitchen, I can tell you!'

She did, quite often, but I forbore to say so.

'I'm having a cup of tea,' I said. 'Will you have one too?'

'I don't mind if I do,' she said graciously, attacking the crack behind the taps with renewed vigour.

'Well,' I said, when the tray was ready, 'what's the news?'

'Plenty,' she said. 'Our Minnie goes from bad to worse.'

'What now? Is she moving?' I asked, my heart taking a hopeful leap. Would Friday afternoons revert to their former tranquillity again?

'Moving? I wish she was! No, *she's* not moving, but that dratted Bert of hers is. He's moving in.'

'But what about her husband? Ern, isn't it? I thought *he* was going to move in.'

'I settled him,' said Mrs Pringle grimly. I remembered her threat of sleeping with the rolling pin on one side and the poker on the other. Perhaps Ern had met his match.

'After all Ern's hullabaloo Bert said his place was at Minnie's side.'

'But that's just what Ern said!' I expostulated. If all the men who had received Minnie's favours over the years suddenly decided that their place was at her side, she would undoubtedly have to look for larger premises.

Mrs Pringle blew heavily upon her tea, creating a miniature storm in the cup.

'Well, Bert's not a bad chap, although no better than he should be, of course, when it comes to Minnie, and no doubt he could settle Ern's hash if he comes back in a fighting mood. So he's gone to live with our Min. In the spare room, of course,' she added austerely.

'A lodger.'

'A *paying guest*,' corrected Mrs Pringle. 'Five pounds a week. All found.'

I was musing upon the expression 'all found' when Mrs Pringle casually threw in her bombshell.

'So maybe she won't need to do as much cleaning work now. I'll find out if she wants to give you up, for one, shall I?'

'Yes, please,' I said fervently.

I poured Mrs Pringle a second cup. My feelings towards Bert, the philanderer, whose relationship with Minnie I had hitherto deplored, became suddenly much warmer. When it came down to brass tacks – Minnie's moral welfare versus my self-preservation – the latter won hands down.

As always, the holidays rushed by at twice the speed of term-time, reminding me of vague wisps of Einstein's theory of relativity which was once explained to me at Cambridge and involved something to do with Wordsworth's 'Ode on Intimations of Immortality from Recollections of Early Childhood'. I may have taken in one hundredth of the explanation at the time, but now I remember nothing clearly, except the fact that things are not what they seem. Certainly, this time business is purely relative, and I give Einstein points for that.

Hilary Norman was there in the infants' room, looking remarkably fresh and competent on her first morning, in a pale blue denim trouser suit.

The children, round-eyed, and in an unusually quiet mood, studied her with curiosity. I don't think they can ever have had quite such a young teacher before, and they were enchanted. Later I heard that one of them had told his mother that: 'We've got a little girl to teach us now.'

We pushed back the partition between the two classrooms, to the accompaniment of ear-splitting squealings from the steel runners, and embarked on a full assembly, starting with 'We plough the fields and scatter the good seed on the land' which seemed a little premature to me at the end of August, until I looked out of the window to see one of Mr Roberts' tractors busily turning the golden stubble into lovely long ribs of chocolate-coloured earth. Farmers, these days, certainly hurry along with their work, and the gulls were having a splendid time following close behind, mewing and squawking like a trodden cat, as they swooped upon the bounty below them.

As they sang lustily, and not very tunefully – music is not one of our stronger accomplishments – I thought how small the school was just now. Despite the fact that two new infants had joined Hilary Norman's class, we were two down on last term's numbers, as one family had moved into Caxley, taking four children whom we could ill afford to lose at this critical stage.

What would happen to us? I was surprised that nothing further had been heard from the Office, but supposed that the summer holidays had meant a postponement of any decision. No doubt we should hear in good time. It seemed that the general feeling was that closure was inevitable. Far better to know the worst than to hang on like this in horrible suspense.

The matter was further aggravated for me at playtime when, mugs of tea in hand, my assistant and I roamed the playground to keep an eye on would-be fighters and coke-pile climbers.

Things were remarkably tranquil, reflecting the golden summer day about us, and I was beginning to relax into my usual mood of vague well-being when Hilary spoke.

'I heard that the school may have to shut before long? Is there any truth in it?'

I came to earth with a jolt. 'Where did you hear of this?'

'Oh, at my digs. My landlady's old friend was visiting her yesterday evening, and she lives at Beech Green, and there seemed to be a pretty strong rumour that our children will be going there before long.'

So our affairs were already being discussed in Caxley! Not that I was surprised, having lived in a village and knowing how rapidly word is passed from one to another. Nevertheless, it was beginning to look as though something definite must be heard soon from official sources if so many people were assuming that the matter was settled.

'If it's true,' continued Hilary, 'I don't think I should have applied for this post. It's very unsettling to have a short time in one's first school and then have to find somewhere else.'

I could quite see her point of view. She was beginning to wonder if we had kept things from her, and I hastened to explain.

'Truthfully, these are only rumours, and we are no nearer a decision now than we were when you came for interview. If there had been anything known definitely, you would have been told. General policy is to close small schools, but it may be years before Fairacre's turn comes.'

I felt it right that she should know that the managers were resisting any such move, and that if need arose there might well be a village meeting to find out more about local opinion, and I told her so.

'This far from happy position lasted for over ten years at Springbourne,' I told her. 'It's always a long drawn out thing. I feel sure that your post wouldn't have been advertised at all, if there had been any thought of closing in the near future, so I think you can look forward to several years here, if you want to stay.'

The girl looked much relieved. 'I think I *shall* want to, you know. It's a lovely place to teach, and the children seem angelic.'

At that moment, two children fell upon each other with the ferocity of starving tigers upon their prey, and a ring of interested spectators assembled to cheer them on.

'You spoke too soon,' I said, striding into the centre of things.

August slipped into September, and the signs of early autumn were all around us. Already the scarlet berries of the wild roses and crimson hawthorn beaded the hedges, and old man's beard made puffs of smoke-like grey fluff here and there.

In the cottage gardens, the dahlias made a brave show, and the last of the summer annuals, love-in-a-mist, marigolds and verbena added colour in the borders. It was a time to enjoy the last of the summer, for already it was getting chilly in the evenings, and I had lit an occasional fire in my sitting-room, much to Mrs Pringle's disgust.

I had purposely refrained from asking about Minnie's affairs. The lady still flapped about my premises on Friday afternoons, like a demented hen, and wet dusters appeared in the unlikeliest places. By now I was resigned to my lot and had given up hope of ever being free of her attentions.

But one afternoon, Mrs Pringle accosted me when she

appeared to wash up the crockery after school dinner. Her mouth was turned down ominously, and her limp seemed more pronounced to me.

'Got trouble at 'ome,' she said, 'I'll be off as soon as I've done the pots.'

'What is it? Not Minnie again?'

She nodded portentously, like a Chinese mandarin at his most impressive.

'Ah! Minnie it is! That girl and them kids of hers come up my place just now, because Ern's arrived.'

'Where? At Springbourne?'

'That's right. She left him cooking sausages and chips. I must say he'd had the decency to bring the sausages with 'im. Probably knew our Minnie wouldn't 'ave nothing worth eating in the house. Strikes me they lives on cornflakes.'

'Is she staying with you?'

'She'd better not. She knows my feelings on the matter. I've told her to clear off home, but she won't take a hint, that girl.'

Some hint, I thought, but Mrs Pringle was in full spate and I was obliged to listen to the unedifying tale.

'She seems scared stiff of that fellow, and I reckons when Bert turns up after work, there'll be a proper set-to atween 'em. Well, I told her straight: "The house is in your name now. You pays the rent to the Council, so your place is inside it." After all, that Ern – or Bert, for that matter – is no more than paying guests, only they don't pay, and if Minnie would only stand her ground, she could get rid of both of them.'

'But will she?' I managed to slip in, as Mrs Pringle drew breath.

'You may well ask,' said Mrs Pringle, unrolling a flowered overall and donning it ready for her session at the sink. 'Sometimes I wonders,' she went on, 'if our Minnie is quite right in the head, I really do.'

I could have told her, but common civility kept me silent.

PART THREE

Fate Lends a Hand

*   *   *

15. TWO LADIES IN TROUBLE

Autumn is one of the loveliest times at Fairacre. We are not as wooded as Beech Green, but small copses at the foot of the downs turn to bronze and gold as soon as the first frosts come, and the tall elm trees near the school send their lemon-yellow leaves fluttering down. A few sturdy oak trees rise from the neighbouring hedges, and these are the last to turn, but when they do, usually sometime in November, their colour is superb.

Now the children arrive with poisonous-looking toadstools for the nature table, and sprays of blackberries, mostly hard and red fruits remaining, as the juicy black ones have vanished down young throats on the way.

We do well for nuts, too, in this area, and walnuts from cottage gardens, sweet chestnuts and beech nuts from the woods, and hazel nuts from the hedgerows also find their way to school. Horse chestnuts, of course, are put to more vigorous use, and the strings of conkers lie coiled on the long desk at the side of the classroom, awaiting their owners at playtime.

This year we were lucky enough to have a sunny October, with those peculiarly clear skies of autumn which show up the glory of blazing leaves. We took a great many nature walks, watching the flocks of rooks stabbing the newly ploughed furrows for worms and leatherjackets, and noting the starlings, excited and chattering as they wheeled around the sky, the flock getting larger and larger until they decided it was time to set off to their chosen roost.

The swallows had already gone, of course. During September, they had perched upon telegraph wires in the village, preening themselves and twittering noisily, preparing for their flight of thousands of miles to warmer sunshine than Fairacre could provide.

In village gardens, the first bonfires were appearing, and wreaths of blue smoke scented the air with the true essence of autumn. Mr Willet was already planning where to plant his broad beans: 'You can't beat Aqua-Dulce Long-pod for planting in November,' he assured me. 'A good sturdy grower, and it beats that blighted black fly if it gets a fair start.'

The holidaymakers were back from exotic climes, and comparing notes on the beauties of Spain and Italy, and the price of a cup of coffee in Paris and St Mark's Square, Venice. These people, of course, were the more leisured among us. Most of us had taken our breaks, if any, in July or August, ready for the new school year.

I was invited to a cheese and wine party at the Mawnes. Proceeds were to go to the Royal Society for the Protection of Birds, of which both Mawnes were strong supporters. As the house is a lovely Queen Anne specimen, and the furniture is a joy to behold, I walked along the village that evening with more than usual pleasure. The older I get the less I want to leave my own home in the evenings, particularly bleak ones, but it was pleasant to stroll through the gentle darkness, catching sight of the various village cats setting off on their hunting expeditions, and savouring the whiff of bonfires still hanging upon the quiet air.

The house was ablaze with lights, and more than a dozen cars were lined up in the drive. I was glad I had not brought mine to add to the congestion. Far too often I have been the poor wretch penned in behind some glossy monster whose owner always seems to be the last to leave.

The village appeared to have turned out in force, and I was soon going the rounds, glass in hand, meeting Mary and Margaret Waters, two elderly spinsters of whom I am very fond, the Lambs from the Post Office, with Mr Lamb's brother from America and his wife, the Hales from Tyler's Row, a comparative newcomer, Miss Quinn, with her landlady Joan Benson, and a host of other friends.

Mrs Mawne, resplendent in black and gold, introduced me to a middle-aged man called Cecil Richards.

'A fellow ornithologist of Henry's,' explained Mrs Mawne. 'Well more than that really. Sissle here has just had a book published. About fishing, isn't it?'

'Yes, indeed. *With Rod in Rutland* is the title.'

I said I must look out for it.

'And Sissle has had others published,' said Mrs Mawne proudly. 'Wasn't *Beagling in Bucks* the last one?'

'No. *Hunting in Hereford*,' replied Cecil reprovingly.

I felt tempted to ask when *Winkling in Wilts* was coming out, but restrained my flippancy. Obviously, this particular writer took his work seriously, unlike Basil Bradley, our local novelist, who turns out a well-written book a year with a Regency buck as hero and a score of gorgeous girls with ringlets and fans. He aims to entertain, and makes no secret of it.

'You must find writing very hard work,' I said politely.

'Not at all. I find it pleasantly relaxing.'

I remembered reading that: 'Anyone who claims to write

easily must be either a terrible writer or a terrible liar,' but naturally did not quote this to Cecil Richards.

'Ah,' said Mrs Mawne, 'here comes Diana Hale. I know she wants to meet Sissle.'

I bowed away gratefully, only to find that I was in the midst of a three-cornered discussion on holidays.

'You really need a couple of years in Florence to see it properly,' Henry Mawne was saying to Mrs Partridge. 'Did you see Michelangelo's house?'

'We saw his "David",' replied Mrs Partridge.

'Well, naturally,' said Henry. 'But *everyone* sees his "David". The house brings it all to life. You went to Siena, of course?'

'Well, no. We didn't have time.'

'Siena is a *must*,' said Joan Benson. 'I think I really enjoyed Siena more than Florence itself. Those beautiful Duccios in the museum by the Duomo! You really should have gone to Siena.'

'I found the leather school at the Santa Croce one of the most interesting things,' continued Henry. 'I bought this wallet there.' He fished in a back pocket, juggling dangerously with his wine glass, and produced a wallet worn with age.

'Lovely,' agreed Mrs Partridge. 'I bought a handbag on the Ponte Vecchio.'

'On the Ponte Vecchio?' echoed Henry, with horror. 'My dear lady, you must have been mad to buy anything there! You can get the same thing much cheaper in those nice shops near the Bargello!'

I was beginning to feel very sorry for poor Mrs Partridge being batted between the two Florence snobs.

Henry suddenly became conscious of my presence.

'And where did you go this year?' he asked.

'Clacton,' I said, and was rewarded with Mrs Partridge's smile.

Half-term came and went, and a long spell of dark weather, with pouring rain and high winds, set in.

School playtimes became an endurance test for all. Deprived

of their usual exercise in the playground, the children became cross at their enforced incarceration. The tattered comics re-appeared, the jigsaw puzzles, the second-best sets of crayons, and the balls of plasticine, multi-hued by careless hands which had rolled various colours together, were brought out of the cupboard to try to assuage their frustration.

It was uphill work to keep them happily occupied. The first colds of winter swept the classroom, and sneezes, sniffs and coughs rent the air. A large box of tissues seemed to be ex-hausted in two days, and my pleas for them to bring their own, or to bring a handkerchief, fell on deaf ears. The tortoise stoves took to smoking, as they do when the wind gets into a certain quarter, and the skylight, as always, dripped steadily, as the rain swept viciously across the playground.

It was during this bleak period that I received another missive from the Office. It informed me that due note had been taken of the findings at the managers' meeting held some time earlier, and that my own comments were being considered. It was only right to point out, it went on to say, that reorganization of schools in the area was now advancing steadily, and that the possible closure of Fairacre School could not be ruled out.

'Back to square one,' I observed to Tibby, who was trifling with a portion of expensive cat food, much appreciated by the cat in the television advertisement, but not by my fastidious friend.

'Now what?' I wondered.

My problems were further complicated on the next Friday by Minnie Pringle's.

My heart sank when I opened the door and heard the crash of the hand brush against the sitting-room skirting board. Since Minnie's advent, all the skirting boards have been severely dented, and now resemble hammered pewter. I think she feels that the edge of the carpet has not been properly cleaned without a hefty swipe at the skirting board with each movement. My remonstrances have made not the slightest impression, and I doubt if Minnie realizes the damage she is doing. At one stage, I forbade her to touch the hand brush, but that too was ignored.

'You're working overtime, Minnie,' I said.

She looked up from her demolition work, with a mad grin. 'It don't matter. I ain't got nowhere to go.'

I took the brush from her hand and put it on the table.

'You'd better sit down and tell me,' I said resignedly. At least the skirting board was spared for a time, but I had no doubt that my nerves would take a similar pounding.

Minnie sat on the extreme edge of a Victorian buttoned armchair, which, I knew from experience, was liable to tip forward abruptly if so used.

'Sit back, Minnie,' I advised her.

She wriggled forward another two inches, and I gave up. With any luck, her light weight would not affect the chair's balance.

'What's the matter now?'

'It's Bert. Him and Ern has been fighting.'

'Can't you tell them to go? I gather it's your house now, or so your aunt says.'

Minnie's eyes grew round with horror. 'Tell 'em to go?' she echoed. 'They don't take no notice of what I says. Anyway, Ern's gone.'

'Then what's the trouble? I thought Bert was a lodger – paying guest, I mean – so surely you can give him notice, if you want to?'

'He don't pay.'

'All the more reason for pushing him out!'

Minnie twisted her dirty fingers together unhappily. 'It's not that. It's 'is 'itting me I don't like.'

'I thought you said it was Ern and Bert that were fighting.'

'Well, it was, first off. Then when Ern went back to Caxley to give old Mrs Fowler a piece of 'is mind, Bert turned sort of nasty and took a strap to me.'

I thought that 'turned sort of nasty' was the understatement of the year if it involved attacking the minute Minnie with a strap.

'Look here,' I said, 'I think you had better have a word with Bert's employers at Springbourne Manor. Let them speak to him.'

Minnie looked more horrified than ever. 'They'd give 'im the sack, most like, and then 'e'd take it out on me. He's 'orrible strong, is Bert. I'd almost sooner have Ern. 'E never used the strap.'

'Well, you seem in a pretty pickle, I must say,' I said severely. 'Why has Ern gone back to Caxley? I thought he had left Mrs Fowler.'

'She gave him the push, and now he's hollering for the furniture what he pinched from our house. 'E reckons Mrs Fowler's flogged it.'

Despair began to overtake me. Heaven knows, I do my best to simplify my own life, and even so I am beset by irksome complications. To confront someone like Minnie, whose relationships with others are a hopeless tangle, makes my rational mind boggle. Where can one begin to help?

'Well, Minnie, what do you propose to do? I take it Mrs Pringle can't put you up, and you certainly can't stay here. You really must try and get Bert to go away if he's becoming violent.'

Minnie looked vaguely surprised, and wriggled nearer the edge of the chair. As expected, it tipped forward and pitched her on to the carpet, where she remained seated, looking perfectly at ease.

'Oh, I don't want Bert to go. 'E's a good chap apart from the strap. I daresay 'e'll be all right if I gets 'im a good bit of steak for his tea.'

I began to feel somewhat dizzy. This frequently happens during a conversation with Minnie. She veers from one point to another like a storm-battered weathercock.

'Surely, that will cost a mint of money? I shouldn't feel inclined to cook an expensive steak for someone who hit me.'

'Only with a strap,' said Minnie earnestly. 'Could have been 'is belt. Buckle end.'

I gave up, and rose to end the interview. 'Your money's on the mantel shelf,' I said wearily.

She gave me a radiant smile. 'Do just right for Bert's steak,' she said, reaching for the hand brush.

But I got there first.

Not long after this encounter, the village was staggered to hear that Mrs Coggs had been caught shop-lifting in Caxley, and was due to appear in Court.

I could not believe it when Mrs Pringle informed me of the fact. 'But it seems so absurd,' I protested, 'when she's better off now than ever she was! She told me herself that she had never had so much money to manage on.'

'That's why she went to Caxley,' said Mrs Pringle, with a trace of smugness which riled me. 'When she didn't have no money to spend she stayed home. Come she got to the shops in Caxley she was Tempted and Fell.'

It all seemed very odd, and very sad, to me. What had she bought, I asked?

Mrs Pringle bridled. 'She never *bought*. That was the trouble. She *thieved*. As far as I can gather, it was things like rashers and sausages and a great bag of them frozen chips.'

At least a change from bread and sauce, I thought, though no doubt the poor children were still having that ghastly fare.

'Perhaps she just forgot to pay,' I said. 'It happens.'

Mrs Pringle snorted. 'Likely, ain't it! Anyway, she said straight out she'd nicked 'em.' Her dour countenance showed a rare streak of pleasure. 'D'you reckon she'll get put inside? Fancy them both being in prison, at the same time!'

'I shouldn't think so for a moment,' I said shortly. 'And isn't it about time the stoves were filled?'

If looks could have killed, I should have been a writhing corpse by the fireguard, but I was only vouchsafed the back view of my cleaner retreating from the fray with a heavy limp.

Most people, it transpired, felt as bewildered as I did at Mrs Coggs' behaviour, and the general feeling in the village was one of sympathy. The vicar had promised to appear in Court to speak on her behalf, and one of Mr Lovejoy's juniors was to appear for her. Mrs Coggs herself, I heard, hardly seemed to realize what was happening. She made no attempt to excuse her actions, not in any mood of defiance, but simply in her usual mood of apathy. It was all very puzzling.

Our butcher's comments seemed to echo Mrs Pringle's way of thinking.

'She's a poor tool as we all know, Miss Read. Let's face it, she wasn't born over-bright, and any wits she had have been knocked out of her by Arthur. I reckon she got carried away when she saw all the things in Caxley.'

'But she is better off now than ever,' I repeated.

'Yes, but not all that much better off. I mean, she's had a taste of spending a bit extra, and it's gone to her head. When she lives as she usually does, it's hand-to-mouth. She comes in here for a chop for Arthur, never anything for herself and the children. To tell you the truth, I've often given her meat scraps and told her to make a stew or a pudding, but it's my belief she doesn't know how to cook at all. How they manage I can't think.'

Another customer arrived, and we were forced to terminate our conversation, but it gave me food for thought.

We all agreed that as this was a first offence, imprisonment surely was out of the question, although Mr Roberts with unusual severity, said it might be an example to other light-fingered neighbours. However, as we heard later, twenty or so sheep belonging to him had that night been stolen from the downs, within two miles of his home, and naturally his judgement was coloured by his loss.

'And if she's fined, then who is to pay it?' asked another. 'The Social Security people? Meaning us?'

'She might just get a ticking-off,' said one hopeful. 'That

Colonel Austin's got a sharp tongue they tells me, specially with poachers.'

'She might get a conditional discharge,' said Mr Lamb, with such authority that his few customers awaiting their pensions or postage stamps began to wonder if he had first-hand knowledge of Courts and their procedure.

It was thus that we anticipated the Court's decision. Meanwhile, we had to wait and hope that, when the time came, Mrs Coggs' case would evoke mercy as well as justice from the Bench.

16. Snow

The end of the Christmas term came suddenly upon us, and we were caught up in a whirl of parties, concerts, and carol services. Added to these school and village activities were the personal ones of shopping for Christmas presents, trying to find out the correct time to post parcels to friends overseas, and stocking the larder for what looked like being the longest public holiday on record.

'You wouldn't think the country was dead broke,' commented Peter Hale acidly, when I met him in the village street, 'when you hear that the local factories are closing until January 4th or roundabout.'

I found myself buying mounds of food against the siege, and having considerable difficulty in packing it away. Does everyone, I wondered, as I stacked away tins of this and that, imagine that starving families are going to arrive after all the shops have shut, and will be obliged to stay for days because of sudden blizzards? I always over-estimate my own – and my imaginary visitors' – needs, at these times, and never learn my lesson.

Because of this unwanted bustle, the question of the closure of Fairacre School seemed to be in a state of suspended animation, and I was relieved to have something else to worry over.

But, all too soon, the festivities were over, the Christmas decorations were taken down, I continued to eat left-overs and term started.

It was quite apparent that we were in for a bleak spell of weather. The wind had whipped round to the north-east, and every night brought us frost. The ground was sodden after the heavy rains of autumn, and long puddles in the furrows froze into hard ice. At the sides of the lanes of Fairacre more ice lay in the gutters, and the children had a wonderful time making slides on their way to school.

'Cruel weather,' said Mr Willet. 'My greens look fair shrammed. What with the weather, and the pigeons, and all them other birds, I sometimes wonder why I bothers to grow them. If I had my way I'd stick to root crops, but my old woman says we must have a bit of winter greens, so I doos my best. 'Tis a thankless task though, when the winter's like this.'

'As long as we don't get snow,' I said.

Mr Willet looked surprised. 'Snow?' he echoed. 'You'll get that aplenty, my dear, and afore the week's out too.'

As usual, he was right.

It began during the dinner hour, while the children were tearing about digesting, I hoped, steak and kidney pie and pink blancmange. Hilary was on playground duty, and I was cutting up painting paper for the afternoon session, when the class-room door burst open to reveal a knot of panting children, proudly displaying the spatters of snow on their clothes.

'Snowing, miss! Ennit lovely? It's snowing! And it's laying too.'

They were much too excited to have understood the different uses of the verbs 'to lie' and 'to lay', and anyway I have almost given up hope of any success in that direction.

I contented myself with telling them to let Miss Norman know that they must all come in to school. They clanged over the door scraper with enough noise for a mechanized army, and I went to the window to see the worst.

The snowflakes were coming down in great flurries, whirling and turning until the eyes of the beholder were dazzled. The icy playground was white already, and the branches of the elm trees would soon carry an edging of snow several inches deep. Across the playground, sitting inside the window of my dining-room, I could see Tibby watching the twirling flakes as interestedly as I was doing.

The snow hissed against the glass, but that sibilant sound was soon drowned in the stamping of feet in the lobby and the excited voices of the children. I could see we were in for a boisterous afternoon. Wind is bad enough for raising children's spirits to manic level. Snow is even more potent a force.

I judged it best to give out the paints and paper as soon as the register had been called, for it was quite apparent that my voice could never compete with the drama that was going on outside the windows.

'You can paint a snow scene,' I said, working on the principle that if you can't beat your rival you join him.

'What like?' said Ernest.

Our Fairacre children are chary of anything involving the imagination. If I had told them to paint the tasteful arrangement of dried flowers and leaves, concocted by Amy and kept on my desk, they would have set to without a word. But to be asked to create a picture from nothing, as it were, filled them with dismay.

I used to be rather hard on them, refusing to suggest themes, and urging them to use their imaginations. But they are genuinely perturbed by these forays into the unknown, and advancing age has made me somewhat kinder.

'Well, now, you could make a picture of yourselves running about in a snowy playground. Or making a slide.'

'Or a snowman?' suggested Patrick, in a burst of inspiration.

'Quite. Or a picture of men clearing the snow away from the roads. Perhaps digging a car out of a snow drift.'

'Or a bus,' said Ernest, 'Only I ain't got much red for a bus. Might do a tractor.'

They seemed to be fairly launched now, and they began their attempts without too much hesitation. A fierce argument broke out, at one point, about the best way of depicting snow flakes which looked black as they came down, but which one knew were white really, and anyway *turned white* when they reached the ground. Linda Moffat said she was going to leave spots of paper showing through her sky, to look like snow. Joseph Coggs said they'd look like stars then, and anyway the sky wasn't blue like that, it was 'grey sort of'.

Altogether, it was a distracting art session, considerably enlivened by the constant uprising of children looking to see how deep the snow was in the playground. Certainly, by the time their afternoon break arrived, the snow was thick enough for Hilary to consult me about sending the infants home early.

'I think the whole school had better go early,' I replied. The sky was low and heavy with snow to come, and there was no respite from the blizzard around us.

The news was greeted with even greater excitement. One or two were apprehensive because their mothers were still at work.

'I knows where our key is,' said one. 'It's in the secret place in the coal hole. I can easy get in.'

'Old Bert can come in my house till his mum gets back,' offered another, and gradually we were able to account for all the children's safety from the storm.

Except, as it happened, for the Coggs children. No one seemed to offer to have them. Mrs Coggs was out at work and would not be home until after three-thirty. I was not very surprised that there were no invitations from the other children. For one thing, the Coggs had no near neighbours with children at the school. For another, the Coggs family has always been a little ostracized by the more respectable villagers, and I had a suspicion that since Mrs Coggs' shop-lifting escapade, the family was even less popular. So far, her case had not been heard, but as she herself admitted her guilt, there were quite a few who censored her, and her innocent children.

'You'd better come home with me,' I said to the three, 'and I'll run you home when your mother is back.'

They waited patiently by the tortoise stove, warming their

grubby hands, while Hilary and I buttoned and tied the others into their outdoor clothes and threatened them with all manner of retribution if they forbore to go straight home.

They vanished with whoops of joy into the veils of snow which swept the outside world, and I ushered my three visitors across the playground to my warm sitting-room.

I had had the foresight to light the fire at dinner time, and by now it was a clear red glow, ideal for making toast, which no doubt would be welcomed before taking the children home.

Joseph was inclined to be unusually self-confident in front of his little sisters. After all, his attitude seemed to say, I know this place. You don't.

They watched me cut some substantial slices of bread. The toasting fork intrigued them, and I set them to make toast while I brewed a pot of tea which I really did not need, but it made an excuse to pass the time before Mrs Coggs returned.

Their faces were flushed with heat and excitement. They handled the toast reverently.

'Never cooked toast,' announced Joseph. 'Never knew a fire done cooking like this.'

I remembered that the Council houses had a closed stove for cooking and heating the water. But surely, there was an open fire in the living room?

'We never lights that,' said Joseph, slightly shocked. 'Us has the electric if it's cold.'

And pretty cheerless too, I thought. No wonder that the children enjoyed my fire, and their first attempts at toast-making.

They demolished several slices of their handiwork, plentifully spread with butter and honey. Outside, the snow drifted along the window ledges, and settled on the roofs and hedges. It was time we made a move before the snow became too deep to open the garage door.

Mrs Coggs had just arrived home when we reached their house. I saw them indoors with a sinking heart. It looked as sordid, and was certainly as smelly, as ever.

Driving back through the driving snow, I pondered on the differences between neighbours and their surroundings in such a tiny place as Fairacre. I was not comparing the fairly well-to-do such as the Mawnes and Hales, with those who had very little, but people like the Willets, for instance, or my sparring partner Mrs Pringle, who really had no more money coming into their homes than Mrs Coggs had at the moment. In most of the homes in Fairacre, one could be sure of finding a welcome. There would be a fire in winter, a cup of tea or coffee offered, biscuits or a slice of home-made cake, or a glass of home-made wine (deceptively innocuous, incidentally) put into one's hand. The house would be as welcoming as the householder. There would be the smell of furniture polish, the gleam of burnished brass and copper, and a bunch of flowers from the garden standing on the window sill.

It was lucky that Mrs Coggs was in the minority in our little community, I thought, as I put away the car and shuffled through the snow to my own home.

But hard luck on those children!

It snowed, off and on, for over three weeks, and a very trying time was had by all. Mrs Pringle seemed to take the snow as a personal insult directed towards her by a malevolent weather-god, and loud were her daily lamentations about the state of the school floors, and the wicked way the children brought the snow inside on their boots.

It was useless to try and placate her, and useless too to bully the children into greater care. The snow was everywhere and, after a time, I decided that the only thing to do was to be philosophical about it.

'It can't last for ever,' I said, trying to comfort my surly cleaner. 'Look, the catkins are showing on the hedge!'

'Sure sign the spring-cleaning will want doing,' replied Mrs Pringle, enjoying her misery.

Irritated though I was by her dogged determination to see the gloomy side of things, I was not blind to the fact that she was not looking at all well. One day I ventured to comment on it. Was she still dieting?

She gave a grunt. 'I lost two pounds last month, and even that never pleased Dr Martin. He's a hard taskmaster that one. I wouldn't care to be under the knife when he's holding the handle. "Got no feelings," I told him straight, I get the stummer-cake something awful some nights, but he only laughs when I tell him.'

'Perhaps you are doing too much,' I said, in an unguarded moment.

Mrs Pringle rose to the bait beautifully. 'Of course, I'm doing too much! It's me nature. "You're a giver, not a taker, my girl," my old mother used to say, and I fair gets wore out. What with this 'ere school to keep clean – well, *try* to keep clean would be truer – and our Minnie driving me mad and the worry over this place closing next year—'

'Closing next year?' I echoed in astonishment. 'Who told you that?'

Mrs Pringle looked surprised in her turn. 'Why, it's general knowledge in the village! And at Beech Green, and at Caxley, come to that. Why else are they havin' new buildings at Mr Annett's? And what about that managers' meeting? I tell you, Miss Read, you must be the last person to know. It's the talk of the parish, and a fine old rumpus there's going to be before long!'

I gazed at her, speechless with dismay. All my old worries, suspended for some weeks, and ignored because of more pressing claims on my time, now flocked back to haunt me, like so many evil birds.

'So it's no wonder I'm not meself,' continued Mrs Pringle, with some satisfaction. 'I can feel meself growing old afore my time. It's as much as I can do to get round my own housework these days, let alone this lot. You'll see my place looking like Mrs Coggs' before long, I shouldn't wonder.'

'Never!' I said, finding my voice.

'Which reminds me,' said my cleaner, picking a piece of squashed clay from the front desk, 'that silly woman's been in Court, and got to go again in three weeks.'

'Why?'

'Them magistrates want reports on her before passing sentence. At least that's what the *Caxley Chronicle* said.' She snorted with disgust. 'Reports! I ask you! I could have given 'em a report on Mrs Coggs, on the spot. It wouldn't have needed three weeks, if I'd been consulted!'

She straightened up and went, limping pathetically, to the lobby.

'Bring any more of that dratted snow in here,' I heard her shout threateningly, 'and I'll larrup the lot of you!'

'Can't help it,' Patrick shouted back impudently. 'And anyway, it's started again, so there'll be lots more, for days and days and days!'

He sounded exceedingly happy about it, Mrs Pringle's

rumblings could be heard in answer, but I could not catch the exact words.

Above the turmoil Patrick's clear treble rang out triumphantly. 'And anyway, I likes it!'

17. RENEWED FEARS

The Court at Caxley meets twice a week, and Mrs Coggs duly appeared three weeks after her first attendance.

The vicar had promised to escort her, and to make himself available to speak on her behalf, should the magistrates so allow, but on the very day of the hearing Mr Partridge was stricken with gastric influenza, and was obliged to keep to his bed.

Mrs Partridge, having left various drinks and some very unpleasant medicine on the bedside table, left the patient and collected Mrs Coggs herself. The vicar, ill as he was, nevertheless struggled into an upright position for long enough to write a letter to the Court expressing his view on Mrs Coggs' hitherto blameless character, and his apologies for absence.

Armed with this, Mrs Partridge entered the annexe to the Court and prepared to wait indefinitely with her luckless companion.

When the case was called, Mrs Coggs faced the Bench with apathetic bewilderment, and Mrs Partridge sat at the back, feeling over-awed by the general solemnity.

Reports were handed up to the magistrates by the probation officer, and silence reigned as they perused them. Every now and again old Miss Dewbury gave a snort of disgust. Her fellow-magistrates were quite used to this. It did not express shock at the facts presented by the probation officer, but simply impatience with such dreadful phrases as 'peer group', 'siblings' and 'meaningful relationship' with which such reports are invariably sprinkled, and which drove Miss Dewbury, as a lover of plain English, near to despair.

Mrs Partridge gave the vicar's letter to the usher, who duly gave it to the clerk, who gave it to the magistrates, to add to their papers.

At length, Colonel Austin rose saying gruffly: 'The Bench will retire to consider this case,' and the three magistrates, papers in hand, made their way to the fastness of the retiring room. The clerk to the justices, the usher, the solicitors and general public were just wondering if there would be time for a quick cup of hot liquid, from a machine in the lobby labelled TEA or COFFEE but bearing no resemblance to either, or better still a hasty smoke, when the magistrates returned and hope was deferred.

'We propose,' said Colonel Austin to the trembling Mrs Coggs, 'to make a probation order for a period of two years. Just listen carefully.'

He turned over a dozen or so pages of a booklet before him. His fellow-magistrates were used to this delay, and their chairman's growing impatience as he stumbled through 'Taking the Oath on the Koran', 'Conditional Discharge' and other irrelevant matters, and were relieved when their ever-ready clerk leapt to his feet and found the place for him, with the sort of fatherly smile fond papas give their offspring when they have tracked down the collect for the day at matins.

Colonel Austin read out the order in a military fashion, and on being asked if she would comply with the requirements, Mrs Coggs said: 'Yes, please, sir. Yes, sir, thank you.'

'You may stand down,' said Colond Austin, and Mrs Coggs, still quaking, was led by the usher to Mrs Partridge who accompanied her from the Court, closely pursued by the probation officer.

'She got off lightly,' said Mrs Pringle later to me. 'Wouldn't have got probation in my mother's day. I wonder they didn't let her off altogether.'

'It means that someone will have access to the household,' I said mildly, 'and surely that's a good idea. Arthur will be out before her probation order ends, and I think it is a very good thing that she'll be having some guidance then.'

'But what about them things she took? Never paid for 'em!'

'They were returned at the time,' I said.

'Well, I wouldn't want to eat anything Mrs Coggs had been handling,' said Mrs Pringle, determined to have the last word and making sure by leaving me rapidly.

The rumours of closure still rumbled about the village, but I did my best to ignore them, despite inner qualms.

George Annett, however, brought all my fears to the fore again by calling in on choir practice night to acquaint me with a new problem.

'I heard today,' he said, 'that Mrs Allen is leaving at the end of this term. She's only got a couple of years to do, but her husband has had a stroke, and she's decided to give up now. What about it?'

I felt a little nettled. I like plenty of time to consider things. Too much, Amy tells me. Some things are better decided at once.

'What about what?' I said, to gain time.

'Putting in for the post, of course,' said George impatiently. 'It's one of the largest junior schools in Caxley, and very well thought of. Suit you well.'

'I don't think I really want it,' I said, slowly, 'and anyway, after such a small school as this one, I doubt if I stand a chance.'

'Rubbish!' exclaimed George. 'You're damn well qualified, and you know the county want to appoint from their own people at the moment, before advertising. You stand as good a chance, or better, than the rest. You think about it, my girl.'

He vanished churchwards, and left me in turmoil.

How I hate having to make a decision! I have the reputation, I heard once with amazement, of making up my mind very swiftly. The answer is that I find suspense so exhausting that I decide quickly in order to cut short the agony.

Now, here I was again, faced with 'Shall I?' or 'Shan't I?' and very unpleasant I found it. Mrs Allen's school was on one of the new estates on the edge of Caxley, and had earned a shining reputation for solid schooling with fun thrown in. It would be a post which would attract a great many applicants, and I spoke truly when I told Mr Annett that my chances would be slight.

On the whole, I felt that I should be wasting my time to apply. Then too, there was the problem of a house. No doubt, I should be allowed to stay on at Fairacre for a time, but if the school closed, then presumably the school house would be sold when the rest of the property came on the market.

I certainly had no money to buy a house in Caxley, and anyway, would I want one? Oh dear, why did George have to unsettle me like this?

I pottered about distractedly in the kitchen, wet dishcloth in hand, wiping the top of the cooker. The stains seemed worse than usual and I squeezed a large dollop of liquid cleaner on to the top and rubbed bemusedly.

If only I could hear something definite from the Office! It would be disastrous if I applied for that post and got it – some hope, I thought – and then found that Fairacre School was to stay as it was. What a problem!

The stains seemed to be a problem too, and on investigation, I found that I had squeezed a dollop of hand lotion instead of cleaner on to the surface. The stove was not improved.

I chucked the dishcloth into the sink and went to get a glass of sherry. At times, drink is a great solace.

The snow lingered on into February, lying under the hedges and along the sides of the lanes.

'Waiting for more to come,' Mr Willet told me, with morose satisfaction. 'I fair 'ates to see it laying this time of year! Still plenty of weeks to get another lot.'

'Cheer up,' I said. 'There are some snowdrops in bud at the end of the garden, and some lovely yellow aconites showing. And the children brought catkins for the nature table – a bit stubby yet, but cheering all the same.'

'Well, you was always one for looking on the bright side,' said Mr Willet 'Heard any more about this 'ere school closing? Someone told me Mrs Allen's leaving. That'd suit you a treat, that school of hers. Should think about it, if I was you.'

As I had done exactly that for a considerable time, with no firm result, I found Mr Willet's remarks a little trying.

'No, I haven't heard any more,' I said, 'and I don't think I should get that job, even if I wanted it.'

'Well, there's plenty in the village thinks you would, when this place shuts up—'

'What do you mean? "When this place shuts up?" We don't know that it will!' I broke in crossly.

'No need to fly off the handle,' said Mr Willet. 'I'm only saying what's going the rounds in Fairacre. If you ask me, it's time the village had a say in this business. It's fair upsetting for us all, and we don't want to see you go. You knows that.'

I began to feel ashamed of my rudeness, and apologized.

'Oh, don't you let that trouble you,' replied Mr Willet easily. 'It's a worrying time, especially for you, and at a funny age.'

And on this unsatisfactory note he left me.

The vicar appeared at playtime, and I took him across the playground, dodging boisterous children in full flight, to have a cup of coffee while Hilary coped with playground duty.

The gastric influenza, which had prostrated him at the time of Mrs Coggs' Court appearance, had left him looking remarkably pale and shaky, and he seemed glad to put his moulting leopard skin gloves on the table beside the chair, and sip hot coffee. Tibby, unused to mid-morning visitors, graciously climbed on to his lap and purred a welcome.

'You really have the gift of making a proper home,' smiled Mr Partridge. 'And, of course, a cat is absolutely essential to that. I hope you'll be here for many, many years.'

'It rather depends on the county,' I told him. 'If only we knew!'

'It's about that that I've come,' said the vicar. My heart sank. Had he, as chairman of the managers, heard at last?

'I've no further news from the Office,' he said, and my heart started beating again, 'but there are so many rumours and conjectures going round the village that I've had a word with the other managers, and we feel we should call a public meeting to air our views.'

'An excellent idea!'

'I'm glad you agree. I feel we should put everything possible before that fellow Rochester—'

'*Salisbury*,' I broke in. 'Rochester was in *Jane Eyre*.'

'Of course. Salisbury then – so that the authority has some idea of the strong reaction to this proposal of closing the school. You'll be there, naturally.'

'When?'

'Now you're asking! It will need to be in the village hall, and what with the cubs and brownies, and square dancing, and Women's Institute and the muscular dystrophy jumble sale and three wedding receptions, it's quite a problem to find a date. However, something will turn up, and meanwhile we must put up posters, and perhaps the children could write a note to take home?'

'Willingly, but we shall have to know the date.'

The vicar picked up his gloves, deposited Tibby tenderly on another chair, from which the animal got down immediately with umbrage, and made for the door.

'So you will! What a wonderful grasp of affairs you have, Miss Read! I wish I were as practical. I think I'd better spend the rest of the morning working out a few dates with the managers, and then I'll call again with the result.'

He ploughed his way to the gate through the screaming mob, and smiled kindly upon one bullet-headed urchin who butted him heavily in the stomach as he fled from a pursuing playmate.

'A thoroughly good man!' I told Tibby as I collected the coffee cups.

Amy called a few evenings later with an invitation to drinks at her house in Bent.

'And stay on to eat with us,' said Amy. 'The rest of them should have gone by eight, and we'll have a nice little cold collation ready, and a good natter.'

'Suppose they don't go?' I queried. 'I've been to lots of these dos – particularly before Sunday lunch, where the joint is getting more and more charred as the visitors all wait for other people to make a move, not realizing that the luckier ones are staying on.'

'That's why it will be cold,' said Amy. 'Please allow me to run my own parties as I wish. Sometimes you are a trifle bossy.'

'*Well!*' I said, flabbergasted. 'Talk about the pot calling the kettle black! You're the bossy one, as well you know!'

Amy laughed. 'I didn't come here to have a vulgar brawl, darling, but I should love a cigarette if you have such a thing in this non-smoking Paradise.'

'Of course, of course!' I said, reminded of my duties as a hostess. 'They're donkey's years old, as I only buy them when I go abroad and get them duty free, as you know. Still they should be a good vintage by now.'

Amy puffed elegantly, and seemed quite content.

'Are you trying for Mrs Allen's job when she goes?'

Not again, I thought despairingly.

'No, I don't think I am. I've been turning it over, and I really feel I can't be bothered until I know more definitely about the plans for this school.'

'I believe Lucy Colgate is trying for it,' said Amy, naming a contemporary of ours at college, whom I always detested.

'She's welcome,' I said shortly.

'She'll be at the party, incidentally,' said Amy, tapping ash from her cigarette with a rose-tipped finger.

'Well, it's your party, as you've already pointed out. I can be as civil as the next, I hope.'

'I can't think why you dislike her.'

'I don't actively dislike her. I just find her affected and a liar to boot.'

'She's very well connected. Her uncle's the Bishop of Somewhere.'

'So what! It doesn't alter Lucy Colgate for me. However, I promise to behave beautifully when we meet.'

'She would have loved this place, you know. She always hoped you would apply for another job, so that she could come here.'

I began to feel decidedly more cheerful.

'Well, she won't have the opportunity now, will she? If Fairacre stays, then I do. If it closes, no headmistress will be necessary – not even horrible Lucy Colgate!'

Amy began to laugh, and I followed suit.

'Tell me the latest about Vanessa,' I said, changing the subject. 'How's that baby?'

'My dear, she's having another.'

'She can't be! She's only just had this one!'

'It can happen,' said Amy. 'It's not due for another seven months. She told me on the phone last night. I must say that in my young days one waited until one was quite five months gone, as the vulgar expression is, before admitting coyly to one's hopes. But there. I gather from a doctor friend, that you have to book your nursing home bed quite twelve months in advance, so I suppose there's no encouragement to be over-modest about the proceedings.'

'I'd better look out my knitting patterns for baby clothes again,' I said. 'I suppose she wouldn't like a tea-cosy this time? I'm halfway through one.'

'Try her,' advised Amy, looking at the clock. 'I suppose there's no chance of a cup of coffee?'

'I do apologize,' I said, making for the kitchen. 'I seem to have forgotten my manners.'

'You must take a lesson from dear Lucy,' said Amy wickedly, following me. 'Her manners are quite perfect, and what's more, she makes delicious coffee.'

'So do I,' I told her, putting on the kettle. 'When I think of it.'

A few days later the vicar appeared, waving a slip of paper in triumph.

'At last, my dear Miss Read! We have fixed a date, though at what cost of time and telephone calls I shudder to think. Here we are! It is for March 1st, a Friday. That seems to be the only free day for most of the managers. Henry Mawne has a lecture on sea birds to give in Caxley, but Mrs Mawne says she has heard it dozens of times and there will be no need for her to attend.'

I remembered how competently she looked after her dithering husband on these occasions, and asked if he would be able to manage without her support.

'Oh yes, indeed. George Annett is going and says he will see that Henry has his papers in order, and his spectacles and so on.'

As George Annett can be just as scatter-brained as Henry Mawne under pressure, I felt that it would be a case of the blind leading the blind, but forbore to comment.

'We'll copy this out today,' I assured the vicar, securing the slip of paper under the massive brass inkstand which has adorned the head teacher's desk here since the time of Queen Victoria.

'Splendid, splendid!' said Mr Partridge making for the door. 'It will be a good thing to see how the wind blows in the village. Nothing but good can come of airing our feelings, I feel sure.'

'Help me up with the blackboard, Ernest,' I said, as the door closed behind the vicar. 'We'll start straightaway on these notices.'

'Good,' said Ernest with approval. 'Save us doin' them 'orrible ol' fractions.'

'They'll come later,' I told him.

18. A Battle in Caxley

Spring came suddenly. We had grown so accustomed to the miserable dark days, and to the flecks of snow still dappling the higher ground, that to awake one morning to a blue sky and the chorus of birds seemed a miracle.

The wind had veered to the south-west at last, and moist warm air refreshed us all. The elms were beginning to show the rosy glow of early budding. The crocuses were piercing the wet ground, the birds were looking about for nesting sites and the world seemed decidedly more hopeful.

Even Mrs Pringle seemed a little less morose as she went about her duties and was heard singing 'Who Is Sylvia?' instead of 'Lead Kindly Light Amidst the Encircling Gloom'.

I complimented her, and was told that she 'learnt it up the Glee Club as a girl'.

It was good to have the schoolroom windows open, although I had to call upon Mr Willet to leave his usual coke-sweeping in the playground to give me a hand.

'They's stuck with the damp,' puffed Mr Willet, smiting the wooden frames with a horny hand. 'Needs to be planed really, but then, come the summer you'd get a proper draught. Bad as that there skylight.'

He looked at it gloomily.

'Useless to waste time and money on it. Been like that since I sat here as a boy, and will be the same when I'm dead and gone, I shouldn't wonder.'

'You're down in the dumps today,' I teased. 'Not like you.'

Mr Willet sighed. 'Had bad news. My brother's gone home.'

'I'm sorry,' I said, and was doubly so – for his unhappiness and for my own misplaced levity. The old country phrase for dying, 'gone home', has a melancholy charm about it, a finality, a rounding off.

'Well, he'd been bad some time, but you know how it is, you don't ever think of anyone younger than you going home, do you?'

'It's a horrible shock,' I agreed.

'That's the third death this year,' mused Mr Willet, his eyes on the rooks wheeling against the sky. The fresh air blew through the window, stirring the scant hair on his head.

'Like a stab wound, every time,' he said. 'Leaves a hole, and a little of your life-blood drains away.'

I could say nothing. I was too moved by the spontaneous poetry. Mr Willet's utterances are usually of practical matters, a broken hinge, a tree needing pruning or a vegetable plot to be dug. To hear such rich imagery, worthy of an Elizabethan poet, fall from this old countryman's lips, was intensely touching.

Mrs Pringle's entry with a bucket of coke disturbed our reverie.

'Well,' said Mr Willet, shaking himself back to reality. 'This won't do. Life's got to go on, ain't it?'

And he stumped away to meet it.

Minnie Pringle was still about her ministrations when I returned home on Friday afternoon. She was flicking a feather brush dangerously close to some Limoges china dishes which I cherish.

'Lawks!' she cried, arrested in her toil, 'I never knew it was that late! I never heard the kids come out to play, and the oil man ain't been by yet.'

'Well, it's quarter to four by the clock,' I pointed out.

Minnie gazed blearily about the room.

'On the mantelpiece,' I said. 'And there's another in the kitchen.'

'Oh, the *clock*!' said Minnie wonderingly. 'I never looks at the *clock*. I don't read the time that well. It's them two hands muddles me.'

I never cease to be amazed at the unplumbed depths of Minnie's ignorance. How she has survived so long unscathed is astounding.

'How do you know what time to set out from Springbourne to get here?' I asked.

'The bus comes,' replied Minnie simply.

I should like to have asked what happened if there were a bus strike, but there is a limit to one's time.

'I'd best be going then,' announced Minnie, collecting an array of dusters from an armchair.

'Don't bother to wash them, Minnie,' I said hastily. 'I'll do them later on. I have to wash some tea towels and odds and ends.'

It would be a treat, I thought, to see the dusters hanging on a line for a change. Their last Friday's resting place had been over a once shining copper kettle which stands in the sitting-room.

Minnie shrugged herself into a fur fabric coat which pretended to be leopard skin, and would have deceived no one – certainly not a leopard.

'Had a bust-up down home,' said Minnie, her face radiant at the memory.

'Not Ern!'

'Ah! It was too. 'E turned up when I was abed. Gone twelve it was 'cos the telly'd finished.'

'Good heavens! I hope you didn't let him in.'

'No, I done what auntie said, and put the kitchen table up agin the door, and I 'ollered down to him from the bedroom window.'

'And he went?'

Minnie sniffed, grinning with delight.

'Well, after a bit he went. He kep' all on about 'aving no place to sleep, and I said: "What about that ol' Mrs Fowler then?" and what he says back I wouldn't repeat to a lady like you.'

'I thought he'd left her long ago.'

'He went back for the furniture, and she wouldn't let 'im in, so he chucked a milk bottle at her, and there was a real set-to until the neighbours broke it up.'

'Who told you all this?'

'Jim next door. He took Ern into Caxley when 'e went in for the night shift. Said it was either that, or 'e'd tell the police 'e was molesting me.'

'He sounds a sensible sort of neighbour.'

'Oh, Jim's all right when he's not on the beer.'

'So what happened to Ern?'

'Jim dropped 'im at the end of the town. Ern's got a sorter cousin there would give 'im a doss down probably.'

'Well, I only hope he doesn't come again,' I said. 'You seem to have managed very well.'

'It's auntie really,' said Minnie. 'She's told me what to do, and I done it. Auntie nearly always wins when she has an up-and-a-downer with anybody.'

I could endorse that, I thought, seeing Minnie to the door.

I heard more about Ern's belligerence from Mrs Pringle, and later from Amy, whose window cleaner had the misfortune to live next door to Mrs Fowler in Caxley.

Town dwellers who complain of loneliness and having no one to talk to, should perhaps be thankful that they do not live in a village. Here we go to the other extreme. I never cease to be astonished at the speed with which news gets about. In this instance I heard from the three sources, Minnie, Mrs Pringle and Amy, of the Caxley and Springbourne rows, and all within three or four days. It is hopeless to try to keep anything secret in a small community, and long ago I gave up trying.

'Heard about that Ern?' asked Mrs Pringle.

I said I had.

'I must say our Minnie settled him nicely.'

'Thanks to you, I gather.'

Mrs Pringle permitted herself a gratified smirk. 'Well, you

knows Min. She's no idea how to tackle anyone, and that Ern's been a sore trial to us all. She gets in a panic for nothing.'

'I don't call midnight yelling "for nothing",' I objected.

'Well, they're married, aren't they?' said Mrs Pringle, as though that explained matters. 'Mind you,' she went on, lodging a full dustpan on one hip, 'we ain't heard the last of him. Now Mrs Fowler's done with him, I reckon he'll badger Min to take him back.'

'Where is he now?'

'Staying with that cousin of his, but she don't want him. He's got the sofa of nights, and the springs won't stand 'is weight. She told me herself when I saw her at the bus stop market day.'

'Is he working?'

Mrs Pringle snorted in reply. 'He don't know the meaning of the word! Gets the dole, I suppose. I told our Minnie: "Don't you have him back on no account, and certainly if he's out of a job! You'll be keeping 'im all 'is days, if you don't watch out." But there, I doubt if she really took it in. She's a funny girl.'

Amy's account, at second or third hand, covered the Caxley incident. According to her window cleaner, the rumpus started sometime after nine, when Ern, a little the worse for drink, arrived at Mrs Fowler's front door and demanded admittance.

Mrs Fowler's reply was to shoot the bolts on front and back doors, and to go upstairs to continue the argument from a bedroom window.

Ern called her many things, among them 'a vinegar-faced besom', 'a common thief' and 'a right swindling skinflint'. He accused her of trapping him into living there, and then taking possession of his rightful property, to wit, chairs, a table, pots and pans and a brass bird-cage of his Aunt Florence's.

Mrs Fowler, giving as good as she got, refuted the charges. He had given her the chattels of his own free will, and a poor lot they were anyway, not worth house room, and if he continued to molest a defenceless and respectable widow, whose husband had always been a paid-up member of the Buffaloes she would have him know, she would call for help.

After a few further exchanges, Ern, incensed, picked up the first handy missile, which happened to be an empty milk bottle standing in the porch, and flung it at his adversary's head. Mrs Fowler's screams of abuse, and the crash of glass, roused her neighbours, who until then had been hidden but fascinated observers of the scene, to open protest.

The window cleaner threatened to send for the police if they didn't pipe down and let honest people sleep and, amazingly enough, he was obeyed.

Ern, still muttering threats, slouched off, and presumably walked out to Springbourne in the darkness, and Mrs Fowler slammed the window and presumably went to bed.

'Obviously,' commented Amy, 'neither wanted the police brought in. I suspect that Mrs Fowler knows jolly well that she's hanging on to property that isn't hers, and Ern doesn't want to be run in for causing an affray, or whatever the legal term is.'

'I thought it was something to do with "behaviour occasioning a breach of the peace"!'

'Comes to the same thing,' said Amy carelessly. 'I feel very sorry for our window cleaner.'

'I reckon Ern is going to have a job to get his stuff back,' I said. 'Mrs Fowler was always avaricious. The Hales had trouble with her when she was their neighbour at Tyler's Row.'

'The best thing he can do,' replied Amy, 'is to cut his losses, find a job, and get Minnie to take him back.'

'Some hope,' I said. 'I can't see Mrs Pringle allowing that, even if Minnie would.'

'We must wait and see,' said Amy, quoting Mr Asquith.

The first day of March arrived, and came in like a lamb rather than the proverbial lion. Balmy winds had blown gently now for a week or more, a bunch of early primroses adorned my desk, and the blackbirds chattered and scowled as they trailed lengths of dried grass to their chosen nesting places.

With all these signs of spring to cheer one, it was impossible to worry about such things as schools closing, and I made my way to the village hall that evening in a mood of fatalistic calm. What would be, would be! I had got past caring one way or the other, after all the weeks of suspense.

There were a surprising number of villagers present, and all the managers, with the vicar in the chair. Mr Salisbury had been invited and sat in the front, with an underling from the Office holding a pad for taking notes.

The meeting was scheduled to start at seven-thirty, but it was a quarter to eight by the time the last stragglers arrived, puffing and blowing and excusing their lateness with such remarks as: 'Clock must've been slow' or 'Caxley bus was late again'.

'Well, dear people,' said the vicar at last, 'I think we must make a start. You know why this meeting has been called. So many people have been concerned about the possible closure of our school that it seemed right and proper for us to hear what is really happening, and to put our own views forward.

'We are lucky to have Mr Win – Mr Salisbury, I should say – here with us, to give us the official position, and I know you will all speak frankly about our feelings. He will, of course, answer any questions.'

He smiled at Mr Salisbury, who looked solemnly back at him.

'Perhaps you would care to outline official educational policy before we go further?' suggested the vicar.

Mr Salisbury rose, looking rather unhappy, and cleared his throat.

'I am very pleased to have been invited to meet you all this evening but I must confess that I am not at all sure that I can help a great deal.'

'Must know if the school's closing or not, surely to goodness,' grumbled old Mr Potts, who is somewhat deaf, and speaks as though everyone else is too.

'Our general policy,' continued Mr Salisbury, ignoring the interruption, 'is to provide the best service possible with the money available. Now you don't need me to tell you that times are hard, and we are all looking for the best way to stretch our money.'

'But what about the children?' called someone at the back of the hall.

'Exactly. As I was saying, we want to do our best for the children, and we have been looking very carefully at ways and means.

'A small school, say under thirty pupils, still needs two teachers and sometimes perhaps a third, for extra work. It needs cleaning, heating and supplying with all the hundred and one pieces of equipment found in a school.

'Now, it does seem sensible to put some of these smaller schools together, to make a more workable unit.'

'When's he coming to the point?' asked old Mr Potts of his neighbour.

'And so, for some time past, we have been going into this question very carefully. There are several small schools, such as Fairacre, in the area, and we think the children would benefit from being in larger ones. Let me add that nothing definite has been decided about closing this particular school. There would be consultations all the time with the managers, and parents too. That is why I am so glad to be here tonight, to answer your questions.'

'I've got one,' said Patrick's mother, leaping to her feet and addressing Mr Salisbury directly. The vicar, as chairman, made an ineffectual attempt to regularize the situation, but is so used to having the chair ignored that he becomes philosophical on these occasions, and really only intervenes when matters become heated.

'Do you think it's right that little children should have to get carted off in a bus, ever so early, and back again, ever so late – in the dark come winter-time, when they've always been used to walking round the corner to school?'

'I think "walking round the corner to school", as you put it, is the *ideal* way. But we don't live in an ideal world, I fear, and we have to make changes.'

'Then if it's ideal,' said Patrick's mother, 'why change it?' She sat down, pink with triumph.

Mr Salisbury looked a little weary. 'As I have explained, we have to do the best with the money available. Now, if we can put these small schools together to make one of viable size—'

'Now there's a word I *loathe*!' commented Mrs Mawne, in what she fondly imagined was a discreet whisper.

'It would seem the best solution,' continued Mr Salisbury, diplomatically deaf.

'Mr Chairman,' said Mr Roberts, who tries to keep to the rules at our meetings, 'I should like to ask Mr Salisbury about something different from the financial side. What about losing a valuable part of our village life?'

'Hear, hear!' came a general murmur.

'We've lost enough as it is. Lost our dear old bobby, lost half our parson, in a manner of speaking, lost our own bakery, and now it looks as though we might lose our school.'

'He's right, you know,' said old Mr Potts. 'And I mind other things we've lost. We used to have two lovely duck ponds in Fairacre. Dozens of ducks used 'em, and the horses drank from 'em too. And where are they now? Gorn! Both gorn! And the smithy. We used to have a fine smithy. Where's that? Gorn! I tell you, it's proper upsetting.'

There were murmurs of agreement, and the vicar broke in to suggest that perhaps questions could now be directed to the chair, and had anyone anything else to add?

'Yes,' said someone at the side of the hall. 'What happens to Miss Read?'

'I understand,' said the vicar 'that Miss Read would be well looked after. Am I right?' he added, turning to Mr Salisbury.

He struggled to his feet again and assured the assembly that I should suffer no loss of salary, and that a post would most certainly be found for me in the area.

'But suppose she don't want to go?' said Ernest's father. 'What about her house and that? Besides, we want her to go on teaching our children.'

I was feeling slightly embarrassed by all this publicity, but was also very touched by their obvious concern.

Mr Salisbury elaborated on the theme of my being looked after, but it was plain that few were satisfied. There was a return to the subject of doing away with a school which practically all those present had attended in their youth, and their fathers before them.

I felt very sorry for Mr Salisbury, who was really fighting a losing battle very gallantly and politely. His assistant was busy scribbling down notes, and there certainly seemed an amazing amount to be recorded.

Countrymen do not talk much, but when their hearts are touched they can become as voluble as their town cousins. The meeting went on for over two hours, and Mr Salisbury, at the end of that time, remained as calm, if not quite as collected, as when he arrived.

His final words were to assure all present that no definite plan had been made to close Fairacre School, that should that situation arise there would be consultation at every step, there would be nothing done in secrecy, and that all the arguments put forward so lucidly tonight would be considered most carefully.

The vicar thanked everyone for attending, and brought the meeting to a close.

'Wonder if it did any good?' I overheard someone say, as we stepped outside into the gentle spring night.

'Of course it did,' replied his neighbour stoutly. 'Showed that chap you can't push Fairacre folk around. That's something, surely.'

19. Dr Martin Meets his Match

Whatever the long-term results of the village meeting might be, the immediate effect was of general relief.

We had made our protest, aired our feelings, and those in authority had been told clearly that Fairacre wished to keep its village school, and why. We could do no more at the moment.

We all relaxed a little. The weather continued to be seductively mild, and all the gardeners were busy making seed beds and sorting through their packets of vegetable and flower seeds, with hope in their hearts.

I was busy at the farthest point of my own plot when the telephone bell began to ring one sunny evening. My hands and feet were plastered with farmyard manure, but I raced the length of the garden to get to the instrument before my caller rang off. Too rushed to bother to take off my shoes, I grabbed the receiver, dropped breathless upon the hall chair, and gazed with dismay upon the new hall carpet.

'What a long time you've been answering,' said Amy's voice. 'Were you in the bath, or something?'

I told her I had been in the garden.

'Picking flowers?'

'Spreading muck.'

'Muck?'

'Manure to you townees. Muck to us.'

'Lucky you! Where did you get it?'

I told her that Mr Roberts usually dumped a load once a year.

'I suppose you couldn't spare a bucketful for my rhubarb?' said Amy wistfully.

'Of course I can. I'll shove some in a plastic sack, but I warn you, it'll make a devil of a mess in the boot of your car. You should see my hall carpet at the moment.'

'You haven't clumped in, straight from muck spreading, all over that new runner?'

'Well, I had to answer this call.'

'I despair of you. I really do.'

'You didn't ring me up to tell me that old chestnut, surely?'

Amy's voice became animated. 'No. I've just heard some terrific news. Guess what!'

'Vanessa's baby's arrived.'

'Don't be silly, dear. That's not for months yet. Try again.'

'I can't. Come on, tell me quickly, so that I can get down on my haunches to clean up this mess.'

'Lucy Colgate's engaged to be married!'

'Well, she's been trying long enough.'

'Now, don't be waspish. I thought you'd be interested.'

'Do you think it will come to anything this time? I mean, she's always been man-mad. Remember how she used to frighten all those poor young men at Cambridge? And I could name four fellows, this minute, who rushed to jobs abroad simply to evade Lucy's clutches.'

'You exaggerate! Yes, I'm sure this marriage will take place.'

'Well, my heart bleeds for the poor chap. Who is he anyway?'

'He's called Hector Avory, and he's in insurance or the Baltic Exchange, or one of those things in the City. This will be his fourth marriage.'

'Good heavens! What happened to the other three?'

'The first wife died in childbirth, poor thing. The second was run over, and the third just faded away.'

'He doesn't sound to me the sort of man who looks after his wives very well. I hope Lucy knows about them.'

'Of course she does. She told me herself!'

'Ah well! Rather her than me. I take it she'll stop teaching?'

'Yes, indeed. He's got a whacking great house at Chislehurst which she'll be looking after.'

'I bet she won't have muck on her hall carpet,' I observed.

'I'm going to ring off,' said Amy, 'and let you start clearing up the mess you've made. Don't forget the contribution to my rhubarb, will you?'

'Come and collect it tomorrow,' I said, 'and have a cup of tea. We never seem to have time for a gossip.'

'What was this then?' queried Amy, and rang off.

Spring in Fairacre takes some beating, and we took rather more nature walks in the exhilarating days of March and early April than the timetable showed on the wall.

At this time of year, it is far better to catch the best of the day sometime between ten in the morning and three in the afternoon, so Fairacre saw a ragged crocodile of pupils quite often during that time of day, while the weather lasted.

The birds were flashing to and fro, with feverish activity, building their nests or feeding their young. Mr Roberts had a score or so of lambs cavorting in the shelter of the downs, and in the next field was a splendid lying-in ward, for expectant ewes, made of bales of straw. Sometimes, when the wind was keen, the children suggested that we sheltered in there, and it was certainly snug enough to tempt us, but I pointed out that the ewes, and Mr Roberts, would not welcome us.

Polyanthuses, yellow, pink and red, lifted their velvety faces to the sun, and the beech leaves were beginning to show their silky green. Friends and parents would straighten up from their seed planting to have a word as we passed, and this brought home to me, very poignantly, the strong bond between the villagers and their school.

Joseph Coggs attached himself to me on one of these outings. He was obliged to walk at a slower pace than the others for the sole of his shabby shoe was flapping, and he had secured it with a piece of stout binder twine tied round his foot.

'Do you think you ought to go back, Joe?' I asked, when I saw his predicament.

'It'll hold out,' he said cheerfully, as he hobbled along beside me. He seemed so happy that it seemed better to let him take part with the other children, and if the worst happened we could leave him sitting on the bank, and collect him on our way back to school.

'That lady come again last night,' he volunteered.

'Which lady?'

'The office one. Comes to see Mum.'

I realized that he meant the Probation Officer. Naturally I had heard from several sources – including Mrs Pringle – that the officer in question was doing her duty diligently.

'She brung us—'

'Brought us,' I said automatically.

'She *brought* us,' echoed Joe, 'some little biscuit men. Gingerbread, she said. They was good. The leg come off of mine, but it tasted all right. His eyes was currants, and so was his buttons.'

Joe's eyes were alight at the happy memory. My opinion of this particular officer soared higher than ever. It looked as though the Coggs family had found a friend.

'We've got a tin now,' went on Joe, 'to put money in. When we've got enough, my mum's going to buy me some more shoes.'

Looking down at his awkward progress, I observed that he would be pleased when that happened. His eyes met mine with some puzzlement.

'It don't *hurt* me to walk like this,' he explained. He was obviously troubled to know that I was concerned on his behalf, and anxious to put me at ease.

I realized suddenly, and with rare humility, how much I could learn from Joseph Coggs. Here was a complete lack of self-pity, uncomplaining acceptance of misfortune, delight in the Probation Officer's generosity and thoughtfulness for me.

I wished I had as fine a character as young Joe's.

Mrs Pringle arrived one sunny morning, bearing a big bunch of daffodils lodged in the black oilcloth bag which accompanies her everywhere.

'Thought you'd like some of our early ones,' she said, thrusting the bunch at me. I was most grateful, I told her. They were splendid specimens.

'Well, yours are always much later, and a bit undersized,' said Mrs Pringle. 'It always pays to buy the best with bulbs.'

'What sort are these?' I inquired, ignoring the slight to my own poor blossoms still in bud.

'King Alfred's. Can't beat 'em. I likes to have King Alfred's, not only for size, but I likes his story. Burning the cakes and that, and fighting them Danes round here. Some time ago, mind you,' she added, in case I imagined the conflict taking place within living memory.

I was still puzzling over the reason for this unexpected present when Mrs Pringle enlightened me.

'And talking of battles, I've just had one with Dr Martin, and feels all the better for it!'

'About the dieting?'

'That's right. Half-starved I've been all these months, as well you know, Miss Read, and fair fainting at times with weakness. And yet, to hear doctor talk, you'd think I'd done nothing but guzzle down grub.'

'I know you've been trying very hard,' I said diplomatically, admiring my daffodils.

'Well, it all come to a head last night, as you might say. Got me on that great iron weighing machine of his, up the surgery, like some prize porker I always feels balancing on that contraption, when he gives a sort of shriek and yells: "Woman, you've gone up"! *Woman*, he calls me! *Woman*, the cheek of it!'

Mrs Pringle's face was flushed, and her pendulous cheeks wobbled, at the memory of this outrage.

'So I gets off his old weighing machine, pretty smartly, and I says: "Don't you come calling me *Woman* in that tone of voice. You takes my money regular out of the National Health, and I'll have a bit of common courtesy, if you don't mind"! And then I told him flat, he was no good as a doctor, or I'd have been a stone lighter by now, according to his reckoning. He didn't like it, I can tell you.'

My heart went out to poor Dr Martin. I remembered Minnie's remark about Auntie always winning when it came to a battle.

'What did he say?'

Mrs Pringle snorted. 'He said I'd never kep' to my diet. He said I was the most cantankerous patient on his list, and the best thing I could do was to forget about the diet, and go my own way. What's more, he had the cheek to say that for two pins he'd advise me to go to another doctor—'

She stopped suddenly, bosom heaving beneath her purple cardigan.

'Yes? What else?'

'Go to another doctor,' repeated Mrs Pringle, quivering at the memory, 'but that he wouldn't wish any such *trouble maker* on any of his colleagues. Those was his very words. Burnt into my brain, they is! Like being branded! *A trouble maker!* Me!'

'I shouldn't let it worry you too much,' I said soothingly. 'You were both rather heated, I expect, and after all, Dr Martin's only human.'

'That I doubt!'

'Well, getting old, anyway, and rather over-worked. He's probably quite sorry about it this morning.'

'That I can't believe!' She sniffed belligerently. 'Anyway,' she went on more cheerfully, 'I felt a sight better after I'd had my say, and I went home and cooked a lovely plate of pig's liver, bacon and chips. It really set me up after all that orange juice and greens I've been living on. Had a good night's rest too, with something in my stomach instead of wind. I woke up a different woman, and went to pick some daffodils afore coming along to work. Sort of celebration, see? Thrown off my chains at last!'

'It was kind of you to include me in the celebrations.'

'Well, you've looked a bit peaky off and on, these last few months. Thought they might cheer you up.'

There was no trace of a limp as she made her way to the door. Discarding the diet had obviously had a good effect on all aspects of Mrs Pringle's health, and we at Fairacre School might benefit from this unusual bout of cheerfulness.

George Annett was buying a sweater in Marks & Spencer's in Caxley when I saw him next. He seemed to be in a fine state of bewilderment.

'Which would you choose?' he asked me.

'What about Shetland wool?'

'Too itchy round my neck.'

'Botany wool then. That washes very well.'

'Not thick enough. What's the difference between wool and nylon?'

'How? In expense, do you mean?'

'No. The stuff itself.'

I looked at George in surprise. Surely, he knew the difference.

'Well,' I began patiently, 'wool is a natural fibre, from the sheep's back, and nylon—'

'I know all that!' he said testily.

He really is the most impatient fellow at times.

'Say what you mean then!' I answered.

'Which wears better? Which stands up to washing better? Is one warmer than the other? Will one go out of shape quicker? Which, in fact, is the better investment?'

I began to get as cross as he was. 'All Marks & Spencer's stuff is good,' I began.

'Have you got shares in them?' he demanded suspiciously.

'No. I wish I had. Honestly, I think I'd choose a woollen one, but some people like a bit of nylon in with it.'

George flung down a rather fetching oatmeal-coloured confection he had been fingering. 'Oh, I don't know. I'll let Isobel choose for me. It's all too exhausting, this shopping! Come and have a cup of coffee.'

Over it, he asked if I had heard anything recently from the Office.

'The usual flood of letters exhorting us not to waste anything,' I replied. 'Not that I get much chance at Fairacre, with Mrs Pringle keeping her hawk-eye on me. She handed me an inch stub of pencil she'd found in the wastepaper basket only yesterday, and she certainly sees that we don't waste fuel.'

'We're going to need more drastic cuts than that,' said George. 'Since these government announcements about making-do and cutting-back and so on, in education, I've seen nothing more of the chaps who were measuring the playground for those proposed new classrooms.'

'You mean we shall all stay as we are?' I asked, the world suddenly becoming rosier.

'Well, nothing definite's been said yet, but I've had no reply to a whole heap of numbers I was requested to send to the Office, "without delay" a term or two ago.'

'What sort of numbers?'

'Oh, footling stuff like estimated numbers on roll if the Fairacre children came along. How many were leaving? How many desks were available, and what sizes were they? How many children could be seated at school dinner? How many trestle tables were in use? You know, the usual maddening questions involving us crawling about with a yard stick, and counting dozens of pieces of furniture.'

'I've heard nothing,' I said cautiously.

'That's the point. It's all delightfully negative at the moment. I think we shall have to hear one way or the other pretty quickly. After all, if the county is going to go ahead with re-organization as planned, it will need to give plenty of notice. If not, we should be told very soon. Either way we ought to know where we are before next term, I should think.'

'Mr Salisbury said we should be consulted at every stage,' I agreed. I suddenly felt extremely happy.

'Have a chocolate biscuit,' I said, offering the plate to George, the dear fellow. Any passing irritation with him was now forgotten, for was he not the harbinger of hope?

When Amy came to collect a second sack of manure for her garden, I told her of my encounter with George Annett.

She looked thoughtful. 'As you've heard nothing definite, I imagine that some committee or other is going into which would be cheaper – to take yours to Beech Green, or to hang on as you are.'

'That shouldn't take long to find out.'

'Well, you know what committees are,' said Amy. 'Sometimes vital decisions get lost in transit between the steering committee, and the pilot committee, and the finance committee, and the general policy committee and Uncle-Tom-Cobley-and-all's committee. James talks about these things sometimes, and what with all the complications, and the Post Office thrown in, I wonder if it wouldn't be simpler to be completely self-supporting in a comfortable peasant-like way with just a potato from the garden to eat, and a goat skin to wear.'

'Smelly,' I said.

'Unless your children can be squeezed into Beech Green without any building being done, I can't see Fairacre School closing,' said Amy. 'And surely, the building programme will simply cease to be, with the country's finances in the state they are.'

'Well, it's an ill wind that blows nobody any good,' I said. 'I certainly shan't bother to apply for any other jobs. I'm glad I didn't do anything about Mrs Allen's. Things look so much more hopeful now.'

Amy rose to go. 'Your trouble is that you are too idle to arrange your own life,' she said severely. 'You simply let things drift and when they appear to be going as you want them to, then you start congratulating yourself on doing nothing. I warn you, my girl, the fact that you haven't heard anything yet, one way or the other, doesn't automatically mean that you are out of the wood.'

'No, Amy,' I said meekly.

'One swallow doesn't make a summer,' she went on, opening the car door.

'You sound as though you'd swallowed *The Oxford Dictionary of Quotations*,' I shouted after her, as she drove off.

It was good to have the last word for a change.

20. RELIEF ON TWO FRONTS

The end of term came, without hearing any more definite news from the Office. The Easter holidays were an agreeable mixture of work in the house and garden, and occasional outings with Amy and other friends.

Earlier in the year, I had been pressed to go with the Caxley Ornithological Society on a lecture tour in Turkey. It all sounded very exotic but, apart from the expense, which struck me as too much for my modest means, I was too unsettled about the fate of Fairacre School to make plans so far ahead, and I had turned down the invitation to accompany the Mawnes, and several other friends, when they set off in April.

I did not regret my decision. My few trips abroad I have enjoyed, and one with Amy to Crete some years earlier was perhaps the most memorable of all. But Easter in Fairacre, when fine, is very beautiful and there were a number of things I wanted to do and see which were impossible to fit in during term time.

Mrs Pringle offered to come an extra day to give me a hand with spring cleaning upstairs. I received this kindness with mixed feelings. Left alone I could have endured the condition of the upper floor of my house with the greatest equanimity. Mrs Pringle however confessed herself appalled by the squalor in which I seemed content to live.

'When did you last dust them bed springs?' she demanded one day.

'I didn't know that bed had springs,' I confessed.

Mrs Pringle swelled with triumph. 'There you are! When I does out that room, I expects to strip the bed, pull off the mattress, and get a lightly oiled rag into them cup springs. That's what should be done weekly, but as it is there's always some excuse from you about "leaving them". Now, Mrs Hope when she lived here—'

'Don't tell me,' I begged. When Mrs Hope, wife of an earlier head teacher at Fairacre School, is brought into the conversation, I just give in to Mrs Pringle. According to that lady, Mrs Hope was the epitome of perfect housewifery. The furniture had a light wash with vinegar and warm water before polishing. Everything that was scrubbable was done twice a week. Sheets were never sent to a laundry, but every inch of linen used in the house was washed, boiled, clear-starched and ironed exquisitely.

My own slap-dash methods scandalize Mrs Pringle, and I sometimes wonder if the spirit of Mrs Hope ever returns to her former home. If so, no doubt I shall see her one day wringing her ghostly hands over the condition of the house under my casual care.

We were washing down the paintwork together one sunny morning when I inquired after Minnie's affairs. I had not seen her on the previous Friday, having spent the day with Amy, and returned just in time to lift the wet dusters from a row of upturned saucepans on the dresser before going to bed.

'Ern's back,' said Mrs Pringle.

I looked at her with dismay. 'Oh no! Poor Minnie!'

'There's no "poor Minnie" about it,' replied Mrs Pringle, wringing out her wet cloth with a firm hand. 'She's a lucky girl to have him back at Springbourne. You can't expect her to bring up that gaggle of children on her own. She needs a man about the place.'

I was bewildered, and said so.

'Yes, I know Ern left her, to go to that Mrs Fowler who's no better than she should be, as we all know. But it's no good blaming Ern.'

'Why not? I think he behaved very badly towards Minnie. Dash it all, half those children he left with her are his own!'

'Maybe. But he's a man, ain't he? Men do go off now and then. It's their nature.'

'I'm sure Mr Pringle doesn't,' I dared to say, attacking a particularly grubby patch of paint by the door.

'I should think not!' boomed Mrs Pringle. 'He's nothing to go off for, living peaceable with me!'

'But is Ern behaving properly?' I said, changing the subject. We seemed to be skating near very thin ice.

'As nice as pie. He'd better, too. He knows he's got a bed to sleep in at Minnie's. That cousin of his give him the push after a few days. The springs of the sofa give way, and she's trying to make Ern pay for the repairs.'

'And is he in work?'

'That's not for me to say,' said Mrs Pringle, buttoning up her mouth. 'There's a lot going on at the moment, I'm not to speak about it. No doubt you'll hear, all in good time.'

'I didn't mean to pry,' I said apologetically. 'I beg your pardon.'

'Granted, I'm sure,' said Mrs Pringle graciously. 'And if you'll give me a hand with these 'ere pelmets, I'll take them outside for a good brushing. They can do with it.'

Term began in a blaze of sunshine, and I returned reluctantly to school.

The children appeared to be in the highest spirits, and attacked their work with even more gossiping than usual. I do not expect dead silence in my classroom when work is in progress, as did my predecessors at the school, but I object to the sort of hubbub which hinders other people and gives me a headache.

It took a week or more to settle them down again to a reasonable level of noise, and a reasonable rhythm of work, so that I did not think about Minnie's affairs until I discovered that she was in the house when I returned one Friday afternoon. She was scouring the sink with considerable vigour when I approached.

'You're working overtime, Minnie,' I told her. 'It's nearly ten to four.'

'Don't matter. Ern don't finish till five, and we don't have our tea till then.'

I remembered Mrs Pringle's secrecy about Ern's employment. Presumably, all was now known.

'Is he working at Caxley?' I asked.

Minnie put down the dishcloth and sat herself on the kitchen chair, ready for a gossip.

'No. He don't go into Caxley no more. That Mrs Fowler and his cousin are after him. He's best off at home.'

'Where is he working then?'

'Working?' queried Minnie, looking dazed, as though the word were foreign to her. Then her face cleared. 'Oh, *working*! Oh, yes, he's *working*! Up the manor.'

'At Springbourne Manor?' I said. It seemed odd to me that Ern should go to work at the same place as his erstwhile rival Bert.

'That's right,' agreed Minnie. She found a hole in her tights at knee level, and gently eased a ladder down towards her ankle. She concentrated on its movement for some minutes, while I wondered whether to pursue the conversation or simply let it lapse.

Curiosity won.

'But doesn't it make things rather awkward' I said, 'with Bert still there? After all, they are both – er – fond of you, Minnie.'

She smiled coyly, and removed her finger from the ladder. 'Oh, Bert's been and gone! The boss sent him packing.'

'Mr Hurley did?'

Minnie looked at me in amazement. 'There's no Hurleys now at Springbourne. Mr David was the last, and he sold up to these new people. Name of Potter.'

I remembered then that I had heard that the last of the old family had been obliged to part with the house because of death duties, and had gone abroad to live.

'Of course! And why was Bert dismissed?'

'Pinching things. He had a regular job selling the vegetables and fruit and that to a chap in Caxley. Made quite a bit that way.'

Minnie spoke as though it were to Bert's credit to be so free with his master's property.

'I'm glad he was found out.'

'Oh, he wouldn't have been, but for Mrs Potter goin' into this 'ere greengrocer's for some lettuces, because Bert told her that morning there wasn't none ready for the table yet.'

'What happened?'

'She said what lovely lettuces, and where'd they come from and the man said he got a lot of stuff from Springbourne Manor, and it was always fresh, and everyone liked it. So, of course, she come home and faced Bert with it.'

'I should think so!'

'A shame, really,' commented Minnie. 'He was doin' very nicely till then. Anyway, Mr Potter packed 'im off pronto, with a week's wages and no reference. Still, he done him a good turn really, seeing as Bert's got a job laying the gas pipes across the country, and they makes a mint of money.'

'So Ern has got Bert's job?'

'That's right! Mr Potter come down to me one evening and talked about Ern coming back and settling down to be a good husband and father, and what did I think?'

'What did you say?'

'I said I wanted him back. He never hit me nor nothing, and as long as he behaved proper to me, he was lovely.'

'So you've forgiven him?'

'Well, yes. And Mr Potter said he could have this job, and free fruit and veg as long as he behaved hisself. And if he didn't, I was to go and tell him, and he'd speak sharp to him.'

'Well, it all seems to have turned out very satisfactorily,' I said. 'But look at the time! You must hurry back.'

Minnie began to twist her fingers together. 'I waited to tell you. Now Ern's back, I don't need to come out so much, and I wondered if you could manage without me.'

'Manage without you?' I echoed, trying to keep the jubilation from my voice. 'Why, of course, I can, Minnie! I'm just grateful to you for helping me out these last few months, but of course you need more time at home now.'

'That's good,' said Minnie, getting swiftly from the chair and collecting her dues from the mantelpiece. 'I've really enjoyed coming 'ere. You just say if you ever wants me again.'

She looked around the kitchen, her brow furrowed.

'I've never done the dusters,' she said at last.

'Don't worry about those, Minnie,' I said hastily. 'You hurry along now.'

I watched her untidy figure lope down the path, her tousled red hair gleaming in the sunshine.

Relief flooded me, as I gently closed the door. Long may Ern behave himself, I thought!

One morning, soon after the happy day of Minnie's departure, a letter arrived from the Office in the usual buff envelope.

I put it aside in order to read more important missives such as my bank statement, as depressing as ever, a circular exhorting me to save with a local building society, pointless in the circumstances, and two letters from friends, which made ideal breakfast reading.

After washing up and dusting in a sketchy fashion, I took the letter from the Office over to the school. No doubt another tiresome directive to save equipment, or else measure it, I thought, remembering George Annett's remark.

It remained unopened until after prayers and register-marking. It was almost ten o'clock, and the children were tackling some English exercises, when I slit the envelope and began to read.

It was momentous news. The gist was that because of the devastating cuts in government spending, all local authorities must make do with the present buildings, apparatus and so on. There would be cuts in staff, both teaching and domestic. Re-organization plans were shelved until the country's finances improved.

There were two more pages after this first staggering one. This circular had obviously been sent to every head teacher. But in my envelope there was a covering letter signed by Mr Salisbury, making it clear that there was now no need to have any fears for the closure of Fairacre School, in the light of the accompanying directive, and that the status quo both at Fairacre and Beech Green would remain until such time, in the far future, when the matter of combining the two schools could be reviewed again.

I put down the letter on the desk, securing it under the brass inkstand, and wondered why my legs were trembling. It would have been more rational, surely, to have capered up and down the aisles between the desks, but here I was feeling as though I had been hit on the head with Mr Willet's heavy wooden mallet. I began to realize just how desperately I had been worrying all these months. This, presumably, was what medical men called 'delayed shock'.

My teeth began to chatter, and I held my jaw rigid in case the children heard. Perhaps I ought to make a pot of tea, and have lots of cups with lots of sugar? Vague memories of First Aid procedure floated through my mind, but before I had time to dwell any longer on my symptoms, a diversion arose.

The door was open, letting in the scents of a June morning, and at this particular moment Tibby entered, bearing a squeaking mouse dangling from her mouth.

As one man, the class rose and rushed towards her. Tibby vanished, followed by half the class, and by the time I had restored order my weakness had passed.

Ernest was the last to return, looking triumphant. 'Got it off of 'er!' he announced. 'It run off into your shed. Old Tib's waiting for it, but I reckon it's got 'ome all right.'

'Thank you, Ernest,' I said with genuine gratitude. People I can cope with – even Minnie Pringle, in a limited way – but not mice.

'I think we'll have early playtime today. Put away your books and fetch your milk.'

When they were at last in the playground, I told Hilary the good news, and then went indoors to see if I could get George

Annett on the telephone. He has an instrument in his staff room, a rather more convenient arrangement than my own.

'Isn't it splendid?' roared George, nearly deafening me in his enthusiasm. 'I bet you're pleased. And so am I. The thought of building going on in term time was beginning to get me down. Frankly, I think we're all a damn sight better off as we are. I shall have to lose one teacher, I think – perhaps two – but the main thing is I shan't be cluttered up with your lot.'

I felt it could have been put more delicately, but was far too happy to voice objections. All my shakiness had gone, and I returned to the classroom in tearing high spirits.

It seemed a good idea, bursting as I was with unaccustomed energy, to tackle one or two untidy cupboards, and I set some of the children to work on this task.

The map cupboard is always the worst. Patrick grew grubbier and grubbier as he delved among the piles of furled maps, bundles of raffia, odd tennis shoes, a set of croquet mallets bequeathed us by the vicar, innumerable large biscuit tins 'which might come in useful' and, right at the back, a Union Jack.

Patrick shook it out with rapture. 'Look! Can us put it up?'

It seemed to me, in my state of euphoria, to have been sent straight from heaven to be put to its proper use of rejoicing.

'Why not?' I said. 'You and Joe can stick it up over the porch.'

They vanished outside, and could be heard dragging an old desk to the porch. By standing on it, I knew they could reach comfortably a metal slot which Mr Willet had devised some years ago, for holding the flag stick.

The flag met with general approval when the children had finished their tidying inside and went to admire Joe and Patrick's handiwork. I managed at last to get them in again, and we spent the rest of the morning wrestling with decimals of money.

The children worked well, glowing with the virtuous feeling of having tidied cupboards and desks.

And I glowed too, with the relief which that plain buff envelope had brought me.

That afternoon, when the children had gone home and I was alone in the quiet schoolroom, I opened the bottom drawer of my desk, and took out the weighty log book which holds the record of the school.

I heaved it up on to the desk and turned to the last entry. It had been made a few weeks earlier, and recorded the visit of the school doctor.

I took out my pen, and put the date. Then I wrote:

'Today I received official notice that Fairacre School will not be closing.'

As I gazed at that marvellous sentence, the door-scraper clanged, and Mrs Pringle appeared, oilcloth bag on her arm, and an expression of extreme surprise on her face.

'What's Fairacre School flying the flag for?' she asked.

'For mercies received,' I told her, shutting the log book with a resounding bang.